Meant To Be

Jessica Tondt

eBook ISBN: 978-1-966931-95-9
Paperback ISBN: 978-1-966931-96-6
Hardback ISBN: 978-1-966931-97-3

Contents

Dedication

To my husband, John, for providing me with the
security and comfort I needed.

Acknowledgment

My deepest gratitude to my husband, whose unwavering support has been the quiet force behind this endeavor. Thank you for always being there, ready with help and endless encouragement.

To my family and friends, who have witnessed this dream unfold from its earliest whispers. Your enthusiasm has been the fuel that kept me going through the heartache and inevitable frustrations. Thank you for never letting me give up on the stories that needed to be told.

I am profoundly grateful for my team of editors, who saw the potential in this story and helped it blossom. Your insightful questions and honest feedback weren't just about fixing typos; they were about guiding me toward becoming a better storyteller. Thank you for your dedication and your belief in this project.

To the entire loving and supportive community that surrounds me, thank you for creating a space where dreams can flourish. Your encouragement has been a gift, and I am deeply appreciative of the love and support I've received.

Preface

As teenagers, my friends and I joked about how we could've written *the* book on dating. We were young and certain; our teenage conversations buzzed with theories about relationships. We'd dissect the mating rituals of our high school hallways, the elaborate games of pursuit and retreat. We swore we'd never fall victim to the pitfalls we witnessed, certain we knew exactly what a happy relationship looked like. *We could've written the book on it!* We were armed with the blissful arrogance of youth.

Years passed, and the laughter faded, replaced by a more complicated reality. The stories we once traded as amusing anecdotes began to take on a sharper edge as we navigated our own messy experiences with love. My notebooks filled with the raw realities of dating, echoed in the tear-stained confessions of my closest friends. The confident pronouncements of our youth dissolved, replaced by a sobering truth: we hadn't understood happiness, only the relentless pressures that chipped away at our sense of self. Vulnerabilities were exposed, compromises were made – and sometimes, boundaries were broken. For some of us, this led down a dark path, into relationships that chipped away at our very being, leaving us confused and asking the agonizing question: *Why me?*

This book isn't the witty guide I once imagined. Instead, it's a journey through the eyes of its young characters. You'll witness the tentative first steps into dating, the vulnerability, and the creeping sense that something is amiss. Within these pages, you'll find echoes of that unsettling feeling, that nagging sense that something is wrong. It's a message to anyone caught in a similar struggle: you are not alone. The pain and confusion of abusive relationships are real, and there is support available. Please, reach out to trusted friends, family, or the many resources designed to help.

Chapter One

When I think back to how it started, especially in the darkest days of it, that was what I would tell myself. I was the one who was so bored with the hamster wheel of endless assignments and college prep that I wanted to cut loose. I was the one who wanted to step outside my comfort zone and explore all the things my parents had told me to stay away from. I was the one who wanted to poke the bear and see what would happen.

I was looking for trouble, and I found it.

My fault. It was all my fault.

But that afternoon in October, I thought a little bit of trouble would probably be a good thing. I needed to shake things up.

Before then, I'd been happy with my safe life, unaware of what I was missing. But at my seventeenth birthday party, it hit me. I'd blown out the candles on my usual ice cream cake with my family, and something began to buzz inside me. It had never bothered me before that some of my classmates had climbed rungs on the path to adulthood, having long-term relationships, getting new cars, and traveling alone to the city. But as I sat around the dining room table with my family, just as I had spent the past fifteen birthdays before, I realized I was still, very much, a child. For months, that buzzing grew louder and louder, screaming one undeniable fact:

Playing it safe and boring meant that I was falling behind.

So behind. There I was, almost eighteen, and I'd never had a boyfriend, never even really kissed a guy. Hell, I was so sheltered that even talking to a guy in class made me queasy. If I wanted to grow up, I needed to play catch-up and fast.

Woodrow Wilson High School, smack in the center of

Pennsylvania, was just like every other high school out there. With its bland cinderblock walls and characterless rooms, it wasn't much different than a prison. The halls always smelled like either pine cleaner or the weed someone had snuck into the bathrooms. Walking past the dull, dark green lockers for the thousandth time, I barely noticed any of the other students. I wasn't hungry for food. What I wanted, more than anything, was *different*.

The lunchroom was already full, but since it was October, my friends and I had already staked our claim. As seniors, we knew the most sought-after real estate, and the best tables were the ones near the window, where we could watch those fancy cars as they drove past. Sad to say, one of the highlights of my day was seeing who'd gotten new wheels. It gave me more ammunition to come to my parents with when I turned eighteen—*Practically everyone in class drives to school in their own car, guys. And I can get an after-school job and be more responsible. It only makes sense!*

Not that any amount of coaxing had softened my parents. They were still under the impression that buying me a car would be a waste since I'd likely be going to college in just under a year, and it would only sit in the driveway.

I spotted the shiny, white-blonde head of my best friend instantly. Penelope Watson was the unofficial leader of our little trio, and not just because she had the most fabulous head of hair at Wood Wil. She was also almost eighteen and acted ridiculously blasé about the sleek black BMW her parents had surprised her with on her seventeenth birthday, big red bow included. She'd always been more mature, even when we were kindergarteners, preferring to hold court on the stairs in her pristine designer clothes at recess instead of getting muddy on the playground, like the rest of us idiots in ill-fitting jeans our parents had picked out for us. Even then, she'd attracted a crowd, and it wasn't long before I'd given up the playground to sit at her feet. Some people are natural leaders, and that's Penny. People hang on to her every word.

So I always felt a surge of pride when she waved to me, as she did when she spotted me among the crowd that day. She stopped mid-sip of her giant water bottle and called, "Hey, you. Sit your butt down and tell me where you got that skirt."

I looked down. I was wearing a short, black denim skirt with a loose, black Misfits concert t-shirt tucked in. I hadn't been sure about the ensemble when I'd checked myself in the mirror on the door of my room this morning, but as usual, Penny's approval instantly gave me confidence. "Thanks, Pen. I... don't know. I found it in the back of my closet."

Of course, that was a lie. My mother had picked it up at Wal-Mart, trying to be helpful since I'd told her I wanted one. The only problem was, it was too big, too long, too weird, too *everything* wrong. I'd had to cut and destroy it to get it to look right. And, of course, I cut the tags out so no one would know where it had come from.

She fingered the fabric as I moved past her. "You're holding out on me. I'm sure I didn't see it when I raided your closet last weekend. I dug all the way in the back, too."

Just then, Sara slid onto the bench next to Penny. "I hate trigonometry," she moaned, saving me from having to lie anymore to my best friend.

Though I'd known Sara longer since she lived down the street from me, and we had more in common, since we both were constantly trying to impress Penny, she'd always been a little distant from me. Maybe because it sometimes felt like we were rivals, vying for Penny's attention. As gorgeous as Sara was, with her long dark hair and pixie features, she was always quiet and reserved unless Penny was around to bolster her confidence.

"Are you guys ready to get food?" I asked, dropping my bag on the seat.

"Hell yes. I'm starving," Penny said, rising from her seat.

Together, we wove our way to the food line. As usual, every guy in the second lunch was staring at Penny. I was partly glad and partly jealous that it rendered both Sara and me practically invisible. We separated to get our favorite food—Penny always got a salad, and Sara usually went for pizza. When I came back with my chicken nuggets with honey mustard, an apple, and a cookie, Penny was already there, picking the cucumbers out of her greens, but still focused on my skirt.

"You should totally wear that skirt to the party tomorrow. It's *hot*."

"Yeah, you really should!" Sara added in the midst of fluffing her thick dark hair, glancing up from the mirror she'd propped up against her tray. "Black brings out the green flecks in your eyes."

Penny nodded absently as she stabbed a tomato with her fork. "Totally."

I frowned as I stepped over the bench and sat down, wondering what I'd missed. First, my eyes were a dull, muddy brown. Green flecks? I'd never seen them. Secondly, the "parties" at Wood Wil were usually low-key hangouts in basements when the parents were away. Same lame, immature guys, the same boring trash-talk about teachers. There was really no cause to go all-out for them. "Wait. What party?"

One corner of her mouth lifted, baring a single dimple on her pale cheek. "I told you, didn't I?"

I shook my head. Likely, she'd just told Sara. Sometimes I got the feeling that Sara and I were interchangeable in her life, because she was often telling only one of us something and simply expecting all of us to know it.

"Oh, well, it doesn't matter. My brother Ben's friend, Kyle, remembers him? He wants me to come to this party at D Phi and hang out with him."

This was nothing new. Penny was always attracting older guys, and Kyle was her latest victim. She'd been the first to do just about everything. I envied her courage.

"Right. *Hang out*," I said, using air quotes.

Sara giggled, and Penny shrugged. "Well, maybe more than hang out. But he's cute. I like him, and I told him I would only come if I could bring some of my friends."

My insides did a little dance of nervous excitement. A college party. I'd been uninterested in the testosterone-fueled boys at our basement parties because they were always trying—and usually failing— to act older. At a college party, the guys would *be* older.

It was the *different* I was looking for, so I should've jumped at the chance. But there was only one problem— my parents. "I don't know..."

"Oh, come on, Ava Parker, you've got to! My parents are going away this weekend, so I have the house to myself," Penny said, smiling.

"You're going to tell your parents that you are sleeping over at my house Friday night. I'll pick you guys up, and we can get ready at my house and then head over to Icana's campus."

That solved that problem. Easy. But my stomach still quivered with nerves.

"Yeah, decent plan," Sara said, looking at me, almost like a challenge.

I could just imagine all the adventures they'd talk about at the lunch table Monday afternoon, leaving me in the dark. There was no way I'd let them go without me. I hated lying to my parents, but I could do it just this once. It would be worth it.

Besides, this would be the perfect way to catch up and prepare myself for next year, when I'd be in college, too. "Sounds cool."

"We're going to have such a good time," Penny gushed and proceeded to tell us all about the last time she'd been to a Glow Party at Kyle's fraternity. They'd got wasted and wound up having a fight with Day-Glo paint, the remnants of which she was still picking out of her hair, even now. But Kyle was *so* hot and had called Penny the sexiest girl he'd ever laid eyes on. I'd heard the story so many times in the past couple of weeks I could've recited it myself. It wasn't just that I was sick of her constantly talking about it; I had to admit, I was a little jealous, too.

I wanted to be that girl. And this Friday, maybe I would get the chance.

"Ava, you haven't said anything. You okay?" Sara asked.

"No, I was just thinking that I volunteer at the animal shelter on Saturday mornings, but I guess I can skip it this week. No big deal."

"You go every week; you should be up for sainthood." She rolled her eyes, then linked her arm with mine. "I'm sure they'll be fine with you skipping this one time."

I nodded and forced a smile, even though I knew I'd miss my favorite weekend activity—cuddling the animals at Seagreen Valley Ranch, our town's local shelter. And judging from how excited they got whenever I walked in, they'd probably miss me, too. "I'm sure."

The girls continued to talk about their outfits, but I was quiet, silently willing my heart to behave. I never lied to my parents, but just one time wouldn't lose their trust. They probably wouldn't even find out. And if they did, I wasn't really lying. I *was* going to Penny's house; I just wouldn't be there the whole night.

That thought made me feel a little better. I wanted different, and I had a feeling my first college party would be that... and then some. If only I'd realized that different isn't always a good thing and that one single night could change absolutely everything.

Chapter Two

My stomach was doing flip-flops by the time Penny honked in the driveway.

I'd been ready for an hour, opening the zipper on my overnight bag about a thousand times to make sure I hadn't forgotten to pack my favorite hair products and body spray. But I didn't want to appear over-eager, so I didn't rush out right away. Instead, I casually went into the living room, bending over my mom's recliner to give her a kiss.

My mother was in a pair of fluffy pajamas, even though it was barely eight o'clock. She tore her eyes away from scrolling Facebook. "Is that Penny?"

"Yeah, she's here."

She studied me. "You said you're not going to the shelter tomorrow?"

"No. I told them I couldn't."

Her brow wrinkled for a moment. She knew I never liked to skip my shift at the animal shelter. Those cute furry faces always lifted my spirits, no matter what my mood was. I'd even made the mile-long trek in a blizzard last winter when all the roads had closed down, so she must've suspected something was up. But then she went back to her phone. "Just text me when you want me to pick you up."

"Okay, I will. Love you!" I slung my overnight bag over my shoulder and headed for the door.

"Love you too, honey. Have fun. And say hi to Penny's parents for me."

Right. Her parents, who I'm not even going to see. I suppressed a shiver as I stepped out into the chilly October night, wondering how my mother always seemed to know when I wasn't telling the truth. It wasn't just that I was missing my shift at the shelter; I'd been avoiding her since I came home from school. I didn't want her to pepper me with questions I'd have to lie to answer.

I saw Penny in the driver's seat of her BMW, visor mirror down, slathering pink lip gloss on her pout. Sara was already in the front passenger seat. She powered down the window and shouted over the blare of the radio, "Who's ready to party?"

I cringed and looked back at my house as I opened the door, half-expecting my mother to come out. But she was nowhere to be seen.

Relaxing, I slid into the back seat and said, "Hell yeah!"

Penny pulled the car out of my driveway and made her way through town to her neighborhood, one of the most upscale communities in Seagreen. The houses were all mega-mansions with deep green, manicured lawns and inground pools.

Penny's, of course, was the nicest one on her block, a sprawling, stucco-fronted thing with two distinct wings that looked like some movie star's villa. Her room was insane—she had her own bathroom with a jacuzzi tub and a balcony overlooking the Watson's huge, park-like backyard with an inground pool and cabana house.

As expected, no one was home when we arrived. The sound of her two Chow Chow nails echoed through the vast foyer as they scrambled on the marble floor to say hi. Two big balls of fluff attacked us with excitement.

"Hi, Lulu! Hi, Lola!" I said to them as they jumped up on me, though I could never tell them apart.

"Down, girls," Penny groaned, pulling on their collars. "Be good."

They did as they were told, and she motioned us to the stairs.

The moment we got into her room, Penny kicked off her shoes and put on the Misfits so loud it practically shook the house. We dropped our bags and started dancing.

"Alright, so what did you guys bring? Show me your outfits!" Penny said excitedly after the song changed.

Sara pulled her outfit out of her bag first. She held up a light-yellow tube top and a short denim blue skirt. She also took out a thin, sparkly belt and knee-high black boots. "What do you guys think?"

"I think you're going to be cold, but it's so cute," I said. It was early October, but fall-like temperatures had hit earlier that week, and Seagreen was on top of a mountain, so we always got the worst weather.

She waved a hand, dismissing my comment. "Eh. Once we start dancing, I'll be warm enough."

I rummaged through my bag and dug out my rose-colored long-sleeve shirt. It had a deep V-neck and fit tight, which I hoped would emphasize my curves. "I'm just going to wear my skinny jeans and booties with this."

"That's so cute. I love the color." Sara said, touching the fabric.

"You're not going to wear the black skirt?" asked Penny.

"No! I mean, I brought it, but it's already October. It's going to be too cold out at night."

"Yeah, but it makes your ass look so good!" She leaned over and slapped it lightly.

"Hey, bitch." I scooted away and threw the shirt I was holding at her, then held up my curling iron like a weapon. "Try that again, and I'll burn you."

She stuck out her tongue at me, and we all laughed.

I flopped on her huge queen bed and asked the all-important question: "What are *you* wearing Pen?"

"Well, I was thinking of wearing my black bodysuit with the mesh in the cleavage. That way, I don't have to wear a bra. You know that will just get in the way tonight." She winked at us.

We all laughed, and Sara said, "Good thinking," but I couldn't help but feel uneasy. Penny was always saying things like that, so I should've learned to let it roll off my back, but there it was again, that nagging voice: *Ava, you're falling behind.*

Sara went to the full-length mirror, unsnapped her strapless bra and slipped it off, then whirled back and forth, fixing the top hem of her tube top and admiring her reflection. "You think anyone can tell I'm not wearing a bra?"

Penny snorted. "Who cares? If they do, you'll be the most popular girl there."

Sara shrugged and tossed her bra in her bag, then looked at me. "What do you say, Ava? Want to let your girls out, too?"

I looked down, really not wanting to be a prude. I was pretty flat, at least compared to Penny, so I mostly just wore camisoles. "Well—"

Penny's eyes lit up. "Yeah. You totally should, Ava. We can call tonight our No-Bra Hurrah!"

"I guess," I said, managing a nonchalant shrug. "But Kyle is your brother's friend, right? Isn't he going to get upset if you guys get together?"

She gave me a look. "We aren't *going* to get together. We're probably just going to hook up. And by the time that happens, Ben will be so bombed, he'll never know."

"A one-night stand?" Sara asked. "You hussy!"

Penny shrugged. "Okay. Maybe two. Or three. Or more. As long as it's fun. He's hot enough."

Sara laughed, but my breath hitched. Maybe I was being naïve because I'd never been with a guy, but I'd always hoped I'd meet someone the old-fashioned way. He'd see me in the hallway or on the street and chat me up, ask me on a date, and before long, we would be inseparable. That's the way my parents met—they went to college together, and he saw her on the way to class, stopped to talk to her, and the rest was history. Every time they told it, I fell a little more in love with it. It was so romantic.

But getting bombed and hooking up a couple of times? *Not* romantic.

Apparently, though, that didn't matter right now. It was *fun*, Penny said, and that was good enough.

"You're bad," I said to her, which made her grin like it was a compliment. But my stomach squirmed because it didn't feel like one.

And that meant something was wrong with me, especially when Penny snorted and said, "Whatever. I'm young. I'm not an old lady with bills and a mortgage to pay. You only live once, right? Get it while you can."

At that, she leaned over and snapped my bra strap in the back, and I winced. Not from pain so much as from humiliation. Why couldn't I just have fun like everyone else my age? I needed to let loose.

So I reached behind me and undid the clasp on my bra, then pulled it out of the armhole. When I checked myself in the mirror, you really couldn't tell I wasn't wearing one.

"Good girl," Penny said as she turned the music back up and we started putting our make-up on and styling each other's hair. When we went downstairs and stood in front of the foyer mirror, we looked a lot older.

"I think we can pass for college girls," Sara said.

After telling Lulu and Lola to behave, Penny pushed open the door. But before she went out, she turned around, a mischievous look in her eye. "Tonight, we are no longer high school students. We can be whatever we want to be. But one thing is for sure... we are going to get drunk and meet guys and have fun!"

At that moment, I wasn't even thinking of my mom or the lies I'd told. I was pumped and excited for the night ahead. *Fun,* I said to myself. *Get it while you can.*

"Let's do this thing," I shouted into the chilly night air as we headed for Penny's car. As we neared it, the porch light hit her windshield just right, and I caught a glimpse of our reflection in the glass. We looked invincible.

But I was so wrong.

Chapter Three

"Penny, seriously, just park already," Sara muttered from the front passenger seat.

"Yeah, Pen, we've circled the block like ten times already. Just pick somewhere," I added, looking out the back window. We'd passed the stately stone-and-ivy-covered buildings of the main part of campus, and now we were near Icana University's Fraternity Row. At least, I thought it was Fraternity Row, judging from all the huge mansions with Greek symbols on the front and every window ablaze with light.

I'd never been to Icana before, even though the campus was only ten miles from home. It was probably nice, but in the dark of night, it took on a sinister quality that made me shiver. There were college kids everywhere, walking in groups down the tree-lined street, standing out front with beers in their hands.

The houses may have been distinguished at one time, but now, they looked worn, with old sofas and a tangle of sports equipment on the porches and scraggly, unkempt bushes and lawns. I could hear the steady, throbbing beat of club music, even with the windows up.

"Hello? I'm trying not to have my car wrecked by some drunk college kids. Okay, you guys? So just calm down," Penny snapped.

Likely excuse, I thought as we went past the same open spot I'd seen the past three go-rounds. *She doesn't want to parallel park.*

Still, I kept quiet and waited until, miraculously, a spot opened up that Penny could navigate into. She pulled to the curb and cut the engine, then checked her reflection in the rear-view mirror, shaking out the white-blonde, loopy curls that fell effortlessly down her back.

"Now, remember, girls," she said to us as she wiped some stray highlighter from her cheek. "There are going to be lots of guys there, but the only ones worthwhile are the D-Phi brothers. Not the pledges, not the scrubs, the *brothers*. Don't embarrass me or yourself by just hooking up with any random loser who pays attention to you just because he's older. Okay?"

I let out a little groan. I didn't expect to be hooking up with *anyone*, but it killed me how Penny always had to come up with random rules whenever we went anywhere with her. But I guess it was our fault because we were the ones who always looked to her for advice.

Sara nodded, taking Penny's words very seriously. "But how do you even know they're D-Phi brothers?"

She gave Sara a look. "Usually, it's obvious. They're the hottest guys on campus. They might be wearing a shirt with the letters. But if not, you should still do your homework and find out."

Tapping my fingers on my thighs, I looked around, noticing that most of the people on the block seemed to be heading toward one house in particular, the biggest one on the block. It was a stately white colonial with Greek columns that made it look like a miniature White House despite the peeling paint. Over the door were the symbols: *ΔΦ*

"Is it that one?" I asked when we all got out, trying to keep my teeth from chattering, whether from the cold or from nervousness.

Penny jumped onto the curb, steadying herself in her kitten heels. "Yep. Come on."

Strobe lights blinked in the windows, and the house seemed to be vibrating from the music. As we drew closer, we realized people were standing on the roof. Someone there let out a long wolf whistle as we walked up the overgrown brick pathway to the front door, and Penny grinned as if it were meant especially for her. At the front door, there were two guys in fraternity sweatshirts waiting, beers in hand, looking like lords of their own kingdom.

Of course, they both caught sight of Penny first, and their eyes lit up with mischief.

"Well, who do we have here?" the guy with the curly mop of hair said, elbowing the tall one in shorts.

"Ben Watson's little sister," the other one muttered. "Hey, Penny. How's it going?"

She gave him a flirtatious smile and touched his arm. "Good, Biggs. And you?"

"It's going," he said, but his eyes were now fastened on Sara. Actually, Sara's breasts. In that tube top with no bra, she was looking pretty scandalous. I was about to tell her to pull it up some when he said, "Who do you have with you?"

"This is Sara and Ava. They're my friends," she said. "Girls, this is Biggs."

I said hi, but Biggs didn't even look my way. He was too busy narrowing in on Sara's breasts. The other guy with the mop of unruly curls was now talking to another girl in a sorority sweatshirt. A chill of nervousness snaked down my back. Was I the only one who didn't fit in? What if Penny and Sara went somewhere and hooked up, and I was left in here alone?

But before Biggs could launch into his greatest pick-up lines, Penny grabbed her hand. "Come on. Let's go inside and dance. See you, Biggs."

I exhaled a sigh of relief as I followed them through the doorway. We found ourselves in a room packed with dancing people. They all seemed to be jumping up and down as one cohesive unit, shaking the floor beneath us. The strobe lights cast an odd glow on their faces, making them look as if they were cast in marble. The air was humid and sticky and smelled like beer.

Sara grabbed my hand tightly as Penny led the way, weaving us through the crowd and into a giant kitchen. The lighting here was so bright it felt like a spotlight right on me. Even so, no one paid any attention to me. A bunch of people were huddled around an island, playing beer pong. They roared and cheered as someone apparently made an excellent play, though we couldn't see from the doorway.

"Hey, they're playing beer pong, guys! I love that game," Penny said, boldly working her way closer.

People kept coming and going, and every time, we got a little closer until, eventually, we ended up right in front and close to the action.

I thought it was enough to be there, in the center of things. No one had pointed us out and laughed, and I'd even caught a few of the guys looking at us as we made our way through the crowd. I figured we could call this night a success.

But I'd forgotten about Penny and her motto. *Get it while you can.*

Before I knew it, she'd walked over to the cute guy who was up next. She leaned her body into his and whispered something in his ear. The guy smiled, nodded, and placed a ball in Penny's hand, turning her around to face the game board. He draped his arm over her and cupped his hand around hers. Together, they tossed the ball toward the cups, and just like that, Penny was in the game.

Her ball didn't go into a cup, but I heard the guy behind her say, "Good first try."

She smiled flirtatiously and said, "I want to try again."

Of course, he was more than happy to let her.

"This game is stupid. I need a drink," Sara mumbled to me. I think she was just as jealous as I was that Penny could so easily insert herself into a room of college kids, even without Ben there to help her. "Come on."

We made our way back into the living room. It was easy to find the keg because everyone was huddled nearby, trying to fill their cups. There were full cups of beer set out on the bar. Sara grabbed two and handed one to me, then downed hers quickly.

I looked inside at the amber liquid, suspicious. Not only did I hate the taste of beer, but it wasn't exactly safe. Anyone could've put anything in those cups while they were sitting up there.

Sara lowered her empty cup and started to move back to the kegs, then saw me taking a tiny sip. "Ava, just drink it. It's not going to kill you."

You never know, I thought. But the way she was looking at me, I felt like a leper. "I just have never liked the taste of beer!" I shouted over the bass.

"You're not supposed to like it! Just drink it quickly, and we'll get another one. Come on, I want to get a buzz going."

I tipped my head back and downed the rest of the cup despite the awful taste. When I was done, I nearly gagged, and Sara laughed at me as she grabbed two more.

She slipped the new beer into my empty cup. "Come on. You want to party?"

At first, I wasn't sure what she meant. We *were* partying, weren't we? But then she grabbed my hand and led me toward a door that seemed to have people coming and going out of it. When I got to it, I smelled the dank air and saw the steps leading downward into a cavernous basement.

As we descended, the music grew even louder until my eardrums started to throb. The basement was even more crowded than the living room, and people were gathered around another smaller bar where a brother was passing out more beer.

Sara grabbed two more and handed me another. It felt already warm. Drunk guys were staring at us from all angles. Well, not me. Probably Sara, since it was pretty obvious she wasn't wearing a bra. Her tube top had slid down so far that her nipples were almost showing. "Uh, Sara, you might want to—"

"I love this song. Let's dance," Sara said to me, even though no one was dancing down there. They all seemed to be actively trying to get as drunk as possible or, in dark corners, hooking up. I felt like I had entered a new level of frat party—a dark, secret level that few knew about.

"I don't know. Maybe we should go—"

"Oh, come on, don't be lame," Sara said, grabbing my hand and taking me to an area where we weren't sandwiched in like sardines.

Then she started to move her hips in a slow, seductive way to the music. Thankfully, as she slid her hands up her sides, she had the sense to pull her top up a little.

The first beer was already starting to work its magic, making me feel a little looser, so I took another big gulp. Then another. And then I started to dance, too, not caring too much what anyone else thought.

I knew guys were staring at us, but it wasn't until one leaned over me that I realized he had a familiar face.

"Hey. I know you," the tall guy said, mostly looking at Sara.

Sara grinned. "Biggs, right? I thought you were on door duty."

"I got off early for good behavior," he said with a wink. "You're Sara, right?"

She nodded, and after that, the two of them engaged in a conversation I couldn't hear, leaning into one another's ears as they spoke. I stood there, swaying to the music and taking sips of my beer. It was amazing. Where normally, I'd have felt awkward, with no one to talk to, I started feeling just fine. I kept dancing, closing my eyes and getting into the beat.

But when I opened my eyes again, even buzzed, I realized something that made my heart jump straight into my throat.

Sara was gone. I was all alone.

Chapter Four

Even half-tipsy, alarm bells started to go off in my head.

I spun around the dim haze of the basement, trying to find a familiar face among the crowd. But they were all strangers.

Their laughter echoed in my ears as panic seized my throat. How could Sara just leave me like this? I had to get out. I had to go...

But where? It wasn't like I could walk back to my house. We were miles away from my home. I was trapped.

That thought made my breath catch, and suddenly, I felt dizzy. I blinked, trying to recover, but the room around me began to sway and tilt dangerously.

Air. I need air.

I moved around the groups of students, first cautiously, then more and more frantically, as the thought of passing out in that cold basement took root in my mind.

Just when I got to the steps, though, a guy cornered me. He was short and unattractive and smelled like something rancid, old cheese and Doritos. "Hey, leaving so soon?" he drawled, his eyes bleary and unfocused.

"Yes," I said, trying to push past him. "Leave me alone."

He clamped a hand over my wrist. "Hey. Not so fast."

I tried to yank my arm away, but his grip was too tight. I couldn't. "Let me—"

Without warning, he leaned over and puked on the cement ground between us. I jumped back from the splatter, horrified, as around me I sensed everyone watching. Someone behind me laughed, and another person said, "Gross."

Now, the foul stench rose up, and I *really* needed air. But the guy was standing in front of the staircase, retching again and again.

"What the hell, dude?" a voice said behind me. A guy in a D-Phi sweatshirt came up to him while he was still doubled over and grabbed him by the collar of his flannel shirt. "You know how long it's going to take the pledges to clean that shit up?"

The guy let out a muffled "sorry."

Then, the brother shoved the guy toward me. "Get him out of here."

I took a step away, shaking my head. "No. I'm not... we're not... I don't know hi—"

The brother had already left, leaving the entire basement staring at me and this drunken stranger, thinking we were together. Just great.

But the way was finally clear. Quickly, I side-stepped the puddle of vomit and rushed up the steps, looking for the first door that led outside. I couldn't find it, though, among the tangle of bodies. I wound up back in the living room under a giant wooden chandelier, where people were jumping up and down to the music. The floor vibrated beneath me as I scanned the strobe-lit faces, looking for Sara and Penny.

Suddenly, someone presses up against my back. Hands came around my hips and rested too low on my stomach. I tensed up, confused, and tried to turn around and see his face, but he tightened his grip around my body and leaned into my ear, his hot breath on my skin. His voice was deep, and he smelled like he'd taken a bath in a vat of aftershave. "Keep dancing. I want to feel you grind on me."

He might have been cute, but for some reason, all I could see was that drunk loser who'd puked on me in the basement. More alarm bells went off. I tried to push away, but nothing happened. This guy was strong. "No..." I began, but that only made him pull me closer to him.

 Just then, a voice from behind me said, "Get off of her, you prick."

The guy's grip on me loosened, but only for a moment.

"Mind your own business. She likes it," the guy behind me said.

Like hell I do, I wanted to say, but my vocal cords had frozen.

"No, she doesn't. Get off." The new guy's voice was calm but authoritative. Commanding. Impressive.

This time, it felt as though the guy had been physically torn away from me, but I couldn't tell for sure because, by the time I turned around, it was just two boys facing off, staring each other down.

"What the hell, man?" one said, and I recognized his voice as the one who had been holding me. He was skinny, with a backward baseball hat and baggy jeans.

The other guy was taller and broad-shouldered with jeans and a casual button-down shirt over a t-shirt. He had dark, wayward curls that fell against his forehead and confidence in his stance that made him somehow look older than all the college students standing around us.

Instantly, I felt my cheeks redden. He was *gorgeous*.

I shuddered and looked around. Everyone seemed to have stopped what they were doing and turned to see what would happen next. From the way he carried himself, I had the feeling that this gorgeous guy was used to having all eyes on him.

For a moment, nothing happened. No one dared even breathe. Then, in a flash, the guy who had groped me dove for the other one. But the taller guy easily intercepted his blow, reeled back, and, like a prizefighter, punched him in the face.

Baggy-jeans-guy staggered back, wiped his mouth, and tested

his jaw. His eyes went to me for a split second. Then he just waved me off, muttered something under his breath about how I wasn't worth it and disappeared into the crowd.

The guy who had just thrown the punch had a dark, cold expression on his face. It made me shiver. But then his eyes shifted to me and softened. "Hey. Are you okay?"

For a moment, I was speechless, drowning in those big brown eyes. I'd never had a guy that beautiful notice me. It was a full five seconds before I realized he'd spoken to me, and I managed a nod. "Sorry. Yes. Thanks."

He raised an eyebrow. "What do you have to be sorry for?"

True. My buzz had worn off, and now I felt completely tongue-tied and awkward. "I don't know."

I expected him to turn around and leave, but he held out a hand to me as if we were in a business meeting. "I'm Jonah."

I shook it. It was warm and pleasant, not sticky with beer and sweat, like everything else in that place. His eyes were warm, and he had a little stubble on his chin, but I was too shy to look directly at his face for too long.

One thing I could tell? He was *hot*. Penny and I differed in our tastes—she liked big and muscular, protective guys, which was why she always gravitated to the jocks on the football team. I didn't care too much about physique, but I liked guys who were more studious and preppy. This guy... he was a little of both. He had an air of dark mystery to him, too. And his face was undeniably perfect, all sharp angles, like a work of art. It was the face of a model in a cologne ad, one that begged to be looked at.

"Ava."

He smiled, baring a set of perfect white teeth. "Cool. You need anything?"

I just stood there, staring at him, half-formed answers amassing in my muddled head. *Air. A place to lie down so I don't pass out. You.* How could he act so casually after punching that guy in the face?

He took a step closer and put a hand on my upper arm. I must have been shaking because he said, "Hey. It's okay. He won't bother you anymore. Are you here alone?"

I swallowed, suddenly remembering the two people I'd come with. What were their names, again? "Oh, yes. I mean, no. I mean, I have to find my friends."

"Friends?"

"Penny Watson?"

His lips twisted. "Blonde? Black shirt?"

"Yes. That's her."

He nodded. "Well, last I saw, I think your friend is a little busy with Kyle. But follow me. Maybe we'll see someone you know."

He led me around the basement, stopping every once in a while so he could say hi to another brother. He might not have been wearing a frat sweatshirt, but I got the feeling he was one of them. So Penny would approve, even if he didn't quite fit in with them. He seemed above them, almost too good to be in this place.

We weaved in and out of the crowd, passed by the keg, and at one point, as we squeezed through a narrow hallway, he took my hand to guide me safely and didn't let it go. He was still holding my hand as we went into the kitchen. I liked it. It was almost as if I belonged to him as if we were a couple. I didn't want to let go.

But as the door to the kitchen swung closed behind me, I spotted Sara sipping a beer and leaning over the kitchen island, giving Biggs a perfect view of her cleavage.

"Sara! Where the hell have you been?" I shouted.

"Oh, hey, girl," Sara slurred, her eyes bleary. She was clearly drunk.

I crossed the room to her. "Where is Penny? I want to go home."

"She's with Kyle, remember? I'm sure she'll be back soon. Aren't you having fun? This party is so awesome." She took a gulp of her beer and didn't seem to notice when it dribbled down her chin.

"Yeah, it's great," I lied. It was great that I had met this hot guy, but I was sure he was just being nice, helping the poor, pathetic high school girl find her friends. Besides, everyone around me was starting to look super drunk, Sara included. If I took my eyes off her again, she'd probably retreat into Biggs' room, and I'd never find her. "I know she's with Kyle. Let's find her and get out of here."

"No! We're doing body shots soon," Sara said as she nodded toward Biggs.

"That's the last thing you need," I muttered.

She slapped a hand lightly on my shoulder. "Oh, Ava. Don't be lame. We're having fun."

Lame. I could just hear them at the lunch table on Monday. *We were having fun until Ava, the lame wet blanket, messed everything up.*

I bit my lip, trying to think of what to say to get her to leave when I felt a hand on my shoulder.

It was Jonah. There was a lot more light in the kitchen, almost too much. It bared everyone's flaws, including the pimple on Sara's nose and the fact that Biggs had a receding hairline. I probably looked awful, too. But damned if Jonah didn't look even *better* in that light, as if it all adored him.

"Hey, why don't we go for a walk?" Jonah suggested, giving me a small but irresistible smile.

I hesitated. He was a stranger, but he had saved me from that creep. And it was better than having a meltdown in the middle of the kitchen.

"Okay, but just down the street and back," I said, glancing back at Sara. "You'd better still be here when I get back."

She rolled her eyes at me. "Where else would I be?"

I can only imagine if Biggs has his way...

I followed Jonah through the crowd and out into the cold, clear night. By then, the porch was empty. When we went down the stairs, I fell into step with him on the sidewalk. Fraternity Row wasn't very long and the D Phi house was in the center of it. It was maybe a few houses to a dead end, close to where Penny had parked. Though it was dark, people were everywhere, so I didn't feel too worried that he was going to hurt me.

No, I felt more worried about what I would say to him. The effect of the beer had worn off so I didn't have the liquid courage running through my veins, and now, my tongue felt thick and useless in my mouth. I always said the most awkward things around guys.

I took a deep breath, trying to think of something halfway intelligent to say. But he didn't seem to have the same problem because he broke the silence first.

"So, Ava, I haven't seen you around here. You go to Icana University?"

I was simultaneously flattered that he thought I was older and scared to death that he'd want nothing to do with me if he knew my true age. "Oh, no. Penny just wanted to meet up with Kyle, so we said we would come with her."

"Gotcha."

Desperate for anything to say, I blurted, "Are you friends with him?"

"He's one of my brothers. So's Ben Watson, who must be your

friend's brother."

From his answer, I got the feeling that while they were brothers, he didn't hang out with them regularly. I wondered why not. But then my insides fluttered when I remembered Penny's comment. *Don't bother with any of the other losers there. The D-Phi brothers are the hottest guys at Icana.* "You're in D-Phi?"

"Yep. Since freshman year."

"Wow."

He let out a short laugh. "To be honest, it's getting a little old now that I'm a senior. Kind of over the frat boy thing."

A senior. Four years older than you, Ava. My pulse did a little dance as I said, "So you're graduating soon?"

"Here's hoping," he said, crossing his fingers. "I'm majoring in entrepreneurship because I'm more into my own business now."

"Your own business?" That sounded so mature.

"Uh... yeah. Well, eventually. I don't want to work my whole life for the man. You know?" He cocked a grin my way. "How about you? Do you have a job?"

"No, I'm just trying to get through school. I don't really have time for a job."

"Yeah, I get that. So, what school do you go to anyway?"

I didn't say anything for a moment, but I felt my cheeks flush. "Woodrow Wilson High. In Seagreen." I expected a stony silence after that, so I started to babble. "I'm a senior. I'm so done with this school year, though. I just want to graduate already. You know?"

I thought he would try to get away from me as quickly as possible. But he was surprisingly chill about it. "I get that. I felt the same way when I was in high school and now. You just want to move on to the next big thing, right?"

"Absolutely," I said, managing to smile at him. He was smiling back.

"So, what *is* your next big thing?" he asked as we neared the end of the street. At that moment, I wanted it to go on forever so I could keep talking to him. "College? Maybe Icana?"

"College, definitely. But I'm not sure where," I said, proud of myself for actually being able to converse without getting tongue-tied. "My dad really wants me to go away. See the world. You?"

"My business. It's a distribution start-up, and right now, I'm only working part-time, making just enough to pay for my degree. My dad's a doctor, and he's still paying his student loans if you can believe it, so I didn't think it was right to have him pay my way, too. So I can't put those big-boy pants on and start adulting full-time until I graduate." He chuckled. "After that, the sky's the limit."

I giggled. God, he sounded so mature, definitely a step ahead of even regular college students like Kyle. A thrill of excitement climbed up my neck as he bumped my arm with his elbow, but I squelched it. If my parents could have seen me right then, they would've freaked and grounded me to my bedroom forever.

It's only four years' difference. When I'm 34, he'll be 38. Not so bad. Besides, we're just talking. And we understand each other.

To be honest, I'd never been that intrinsically drawn to any person before in my life. I wanted to know everything there was about him. I was about to ask him more about his business, but as we reached the dead end, someone started shouting my name.

I spun around to see Sara running toward me. She stopped short, glancing between us. "Hey. I found Penny."

As I sighed with relief that this nightmare of an evening was about to come to an end, I looked over at Jonah, who was standing with his hands in the pockets of his jeans. Regret instantly washed over me as he said, "Guess you've got to go."

"I guess," I said, and at that moment, I didn't want to. I wanted to see how this would play out. Would he ask me to dance? Maybe he would try to kiss me. I might have been wrong, but it seemed like he was actually interested in me. The thought made my pulse skitter.

But it was too late. Sara was ready to go. We followed her back toward the D Phi house. "Where is—"

Before I could finish, I noticed Penny power-walking toward her car. She looked the way she had when Mr. Franks had given her a D in Geometry—pissed.

"I've got to go," I called to Jonah, hurrying to the car and sliding into the back seat as soon as she opened the doors. Penny slid in and started the engine, throwing the car into drive with a powerful shove of the stick. "Pen. What's wrong?"

"Nothing. Just that Kyle's a dick," Penny mumbled, turning the wheel and shrieking out of the space before Sara had even closed the front passenger side door. "To hell with this place."

"I thought you didn't want anything serious anyway," Sara said as I looked out the window at Jonah. He was standing on the curb, hands in his pockets, his eyes fastened on me.

My pulse went wild again.

"I didn't, but he's so hot. A hot jerk." She slammed on the gas, going too fast in the residential neighborhood. Jonah slipped from my view. "Oh, well."

Sara stared at her. "So... no two-night stand?"

She snorted. "Not unless he apologizes, big-time. There are plenty of other D Phi brothers. I don't need to waste my time on him," she muttered, her fingers tightening on the steering wheel, and she hung a turn so violently I almost fell over in the back seat.

"I think when we get home, we should bake some brownies and watch that new romcom," Sara said.

"That sounds like a great idea! Huh, Penny?" I said, rubbing her shoulder.

Penny smiled and took her foot off the gas. "Yeah, I think we have a couple of boxes of brownie mix in the pantry."

As we drove back, I thought of Jonah. Nothing would come of that. He hadn't even held my hand. No, tomorrow, he'd probably find a college girl who was prettier and had more going for her than I did. Despite the little flutter he gave me and the fact that we'd connected during our short conversation, it couldn't work out.

And that's for the best, I told myself.

If only I'd listened.

Chapter Five

I rolled over in my sleeping bag as bright late-morning sunlight slashed through the blinds, hitting my face.

It had to be at least ten. Maybe eleven. I'd never really slept, but the girls had, so I spent most of the time staring at the ceiling.

It wasn't that Penny's floor was uncomfortable. Her rug was plush and soft white fur, better even than my mattress at home. I hadn't minded giving Sara the extra space on Penny's giant queen bed, and when I'd sunk under the covers last night, I was exhausted. All of us were, so much so that we didn't bother to make the brownies. I'd thought for sure I'd be asleep as soon as my head hit the pillow.

Instead, I'd lain awake, listening to the girls snoring lightly, tossing and turning, thinking about my first college frat party.

Actually, no. I was thinking mostly about Jonah.

I'd heard so many people talk about the spark. That little bit of connection that you'd feel with someone you were compatible with. I'd thought such a thing existed, but I'd never thought I would feel it because, to be honest, I thought I was too weird.

Most of the things I liked, other people didn't, so I never thought I'd have a true, pre-ordained, cosmic connection with anyone. I thought I'd have to be more like Penny to ever feel something like that.

But with Jonah, it had been easy. In that short moment, we'd connected on a level I'd never had with any guy before.

Crazy, I thought, pulling the top of the sleeping bag up over my shoulders to stop myself from shivering at the memory of him punching that guy out. Defending my honor. So chivalrous. So sweet.

Not to mention, he was hot. How had a guy like that actually shown interest in *me*? Or was he just being nice? As crazy as it was, it made me feel less so. If Jonah had shown interest in me, maybe I wasn't so odd after all.

I rolled over again to stop the squirming sensation from taking over. The antsy feeling was too much. I wanted to talk to the girls about it, but judging from their breathing, they were still asleep.

I'd wanted different, and I'd found it. The trouble was, now that I'd seen it, I didn't want to go back. Now that I'd seen what else was out there, the thought of walking those dull hallways at Wood Wil made my stomach turn.

Letting out a heavy sigh, I climbed out of my bag and stood up to look at them. Still, sound asleep. I made more than a little noise, closing the door behind me as I went down to the kitchen to grab a bottle of water from the fridge.

I took a big swig and paced in circles around the kitchen island, trying to work out the nervous energy.

Really, Ava. Get a grip. He didn't ask for your number. You'll probably never see him again.

That thought made my spirits sink, even as I climbed the curved staircase back to Penny's room. When I got back in, she was rolling over and yawning, which I decided was close enough to be awake.

"Hey guys," I said loudly, unscrewing the cap of my water. "What do you think it means if a guy punches another guy for you?"

Penny instantly sat up in bed. Her eyes were a little bleary, but she looked just as fresh-faced and pretty as ever. "What? Is this a hypothetical question, or did two guys fight over you last night?" She gave me a skeptical look.

"No, two guys didn't fight over *me*," I said, though that

probably would've made for a better story. "But one guy did try to grind on me when you two ditched me last night. He wouldn't let go of me, and this other guy saw him and punched him out."

Sara groaned without removing the pillow from her face. "We *didn't* ditch you," her muffled voice came from underneath. "I looked around, and you weren't there."

Penny fell back on her pillow. "Guys are such idiots. Really? So, who was this knight in shining armor?"

"His name is Jonah. He's a senior and a D Phi brother," I said with a hint of pride.

She frowned. "Right... I've heard of him, but I've never seen him. He's not around a lot. A senior." Her eyes widened with approval. "Is he the one you were walking with?"

I nod.

Sara was up now, wiping the sleep from her eyes. "He was *hot*, Ava. Did you hook up?"

They both stared at me expectantly, wanting details, but it felt cheap to reduce my relationship with Jonah to something merely physical. We'd had more than that. "Well...no, we just talked. That's all."

"Really?" Penny looked bored. "Well, then, I guess it doesn't mean anything. He was probably just being nice."

That hit me like a slap to the face. *Was* he just being nice? Maybe. Probably. After all, I still couldn't understand why he was talking to me. She was probably right.

"Yeah," I agreed with a nonchalant shrug, even though I hoped she was wrong. "I mean, he did suggest we go for a walk together..." I went on, hoping that she would change her mind.

"God, my head hurts. Hangovers are the worst," Sara groaned, rolling over and putting the pillow over her head again. "Did hottie ask for your number?"

I swallowed. I guess that was the test. It was hopeless. I needed to put him out of my head.

"Because Biggs asked for mine," Sara said triumphantly, groping for her phone and holding it up.

"He did not!" Penny said, grabbing the phone and looking at it. "No messages. I guess it's a little too early to expect him to message you. Did you guys hook up?"

She sat up and grinned. "A little. But I don't kiss and tell."

Penny threw her pillow at her. "Bitch, you'd better. You know, his last name isn't even Biggs. The rumor is it's his D-Phi nickname because of what he's got in his pants." She leaned in. "Confirm or deny?"

Sara gave her a mischievous look. "Confirm!"

Penny's jaw dropped, and they both squealed, which made my stomach sink. All I'd done was talk to a guy who'd taken pity on me as a charity case. Of course, they'd dismiss it. It was nothing.

Ava, you're falling behind.

"So Kyle was a jerk?" I asked Penny, sitting on the edge of the bed.

She nodded. "Yeah. He took me to his room and was acting all sweet. And then afterward, when I told him I could come back for the next party, he blew me off. The second we went back downstairs, he pretended he didn't know me and started talking to some other girl."

As bad as I felt for Penny, it made me feel a little better to know her cute college guy wasn't going to be calling her, either. "Asshole."

"Absolutely," she said, reaching for her phone. "But I'm going to text my brother and find out when the next party is. Then I'll find another guy and make him jealous. Who's in?"

Sara grinned. "Cool."

I hesitated. As much as I wanted to see Jonah again, I didn't know how we'd make it happen without another sleepover. "Are your parents going out of town again?"

She waved me off. "We'll cross that bridge when we come to it," she said, tapping on her phone display. "Oh. Look. It's a text from Ben. I wonder what he wants. He usually sleeps until noon after a party, the loser."

"Read it!" Sara shouted though Penny was already opening it.

She let out a little gasp of surprise.

"What? Is it about Kyle?" Sara prodded.

"Well, would you look at that," she said, reading the message, then looking at me. "He says that Jonah asked him to get your number from me."

I stared in shock.

"So *someone* must have made an impression," she said with a glint of mischief and accusation in her eyes. "Nothing happened? Come on, Ava. You're not being straight with us."

Chapter Six

Of course, after that, I was on cloud nine.

My friends peppered me with questions about Jonah, none of which I could answer. They didn't believe that I'd just talked to him for a few minutes. They assumed I must've done something else, something magical, to have captured the hot college senior's attention. But I doubted I possessed any magic. To be honest, I thought he had the wrong girl.

Still, that didn't appease them. We spent the next fifteen minutes trying to think about what to write back to Ben. *Something that shows you're interested,* Penny had instructed, but I wasn't sure that was a good idea. Weren't girls supposed to play hard to get? Eventually, I asked her to just put my phone number in, and leave it at that.

Then we spent the rest of our time together, checking my phone obsessively, waiting for him to get in touch.

He didn't.

But I had to admit, as I gathered up my things and went out to the driveway where my mom was waiting in her SUV, that it was nice to have the girls speculating about my love life. Penny usually occupied center stage in our friend group, with Sara and I fighting for her attention. Sara was sometimes able to steal the spotlight away, but me? Never.

I had to admit it was a nice place to be, and I didn't want to fade into the background just yet.

Maybe this is the start of things, I thought, checking my phone for the billionth time before sliding into the front passenger seat next to my mom.

"Hi, honey. Have fun?" she asked as she checked the rear-view mirror to pull out.

I realized I was smiling from ear to ear and wiped the grin off my face. "Yeah, it was great."

As soon as she shifted into drive, she gave me a closer look. "You look tired. I bet you didn't get much sleep."

I'd gotten zero sleep, but I wasn't about to tell her why. "No. Not much."

"I get it. Girls love to stay up late and gossip." That was true, so I just smiled dumbly. "I was going to suggest you go into the animal shelter for a couple of hours if you were up to it. But you'd better just rest up."

I yawned. Usually, nothing could tear me away from cuddling little kittens, but this morning, the thought made me feel even more exhausted. "Yeah. I'd rather just rest."

"Cool." She pointed the car toward home. "I made homemade chicken noodle soup. It's in the fridge. Just get yourself a cup when you're hungry."

"Sounds good."

But I never got hungry. When I got back to my bedroom, threw my bag on the ground, and shut the door, I didn't rest. Instead, I alternated between checking my phone and standing in front of the mirror, trying to see what Jonah had seen in me.

He wouldn't have bothered to ask Ben if he wasn't really interested, would he? Or was this just a game? And *why* was he interested? I was plain, with long brown hair, and brown eyes, nothing that really stood out. But *something* had stood out to him. Out of all the college women that must've constantly surrounded him, he'd wanted my number. Was it because I was the damsel in distress? The questions practically drove me mad.

I flattened my sweatshirt in the front and stuck my chest out. Hopeless, but I could probably buy one of those bras with the padding. My hair was dull, but Penny always told me I'd look fabulous with blonde highlights. All the girls at school went for monthly manicure sessions and spa treatments, but not me. I'd never really taken care of myself that much, but maybe I should start. Maybe that's what Jonah had seen—a diamond in the rough.

Yawning again, I tried to put it out of my mind and take a nap, but I wound up with my phone in hand, trying to Google him.

I didn't know his last name, so I just put in *Jonah Icana University Delta Phi.*

That brought up a pretty reliable hit from a couple of years ago. Jonah Manzano, Business and Entrepreneurship Major. He'd won some scholarship from a local entrepreneur's group for a presentation he gave. There was a photograph of him holding a giant check, flanked by several men in suits. I gaped at the sight of him and his self-assured smile. He looked so... adult.

Ava Manzano, I thought, liking the sound of it. *My husband, Jonah, and I...*

Then I shook my head at my silliness and scrolled through the next results. I found an older hit, results from a Delta Phi charity 5k, but nothing else.

I collapsed back in the bed, closing my eyes.

A second later, my phone buzzed, and I opened it up to find a Snapchat notification from Penny. *Did he text you yet?*

I sighed. It was going to be a long weekend.

It was probably a game. He was going to wait until I was drooling and half-insane, which, judging from the way I was feeling, wouldn't be long.

Chill, I typed in. *You only gave Ben my number 40 minutes ago!*

She responded with: *You're right. College boys are notoriously lazy. Let me know the second he gets in touch. But I bet you he'll wait at least a week.*

A week? I thought I'd die. *Really?*

Yeah. They don't want to give away their game by coming off as too interested.

Penny definitely knew more about guys than we did, and so Sara and I always took her word as gospel. But at that point, I'd already begun to doubt her little bits of guy wisdom. Jonah didn't seem lazy. He'd said he had his own business. Besides, she'd told us all guys wanted to do was hook up, but Jonah hadn't put any moves on me last night. If that was all he wanted, he wouldn't have gone through the trouble of getting my number. There were any number of willing girls on campus he could've gotten with after I left the party.

I texted her, *You're probably right,* but my stomach did backflips. If he waited a week, I'd probably have an ulcer by then. Or what if he never texted? That would be so much build-up for nothing.

I tried to put it out of my head for the rest of the day, but I couldn't. I checked my phone a thousand times and brought it to the dinner table when Mom rolled out her famous lasagna. By then, I *still* wasn't hungry—my unsettled stomach was growling like there was an alien in there.

"No phones at the table," she said to me as she cut me a too-big square, despite my thinking I was doing a good job hiding my phone in my lap.

"Sorry," I said, obediently setting it on the window ledge behind me.

"So. How was your sleepover?" My dad asked, cutting a piece of lasagna with his fork. "The girls thinking of college?"

I looked up at the ceiling. The girls and I never talked about college because our parents talked about it enough for all of us.

Every time, it felt like a lecture. "I guess they are."

"Which reminds me," my Mom said, pointing to the table behind her, which had become the depository for all the college brochures I'd been receiving. The stack was dangerously close to an avalanche. "Are you going to go through these?"

I nodded. "Soon."

"Good, because it's good to get your application in as early as possible," my father said, wiping his mouth with a napkin. "I'm sure you're going to apply to Penn State, but—"

"Don't forget Icana," my mother added. "You can commute."

My ears perked up at the mention of Icana. But what did it matter if I got in there? Jonah would already have graduated.

I gritted my teeth. *Ava, stop thinking about him already.*

At that, my phone buzzed. I glanced over, expecting to see a notification from one of my other apps. But it was a text.

I couldn't see who it was from, so I leaned over just as my dad said, "Icana's a good safety. But I think college is about spreading your wings. Finding yourself. Experiencing new things, new places."

It was the same song-and-dance I'd heard a thousand times before. He said more, but I was so busy tipping my chair back and scooting to the seat's edge, trying to see the display, that I tuned everything else out. I could almost see the text notification. Was it Penny asking if I'd heard yet? Or... could it be from an unknown number?

Without warning, my mother let out a sharp, "Ava!"

I swung around, and the chair fell forward onto all four legs with a loud bang that made me bite my tongue. "Huh?"

"Your phone can wait until after dinner!"

"If you keep doing that to your chair, you're going to break it," my father said, his tone sharp as he pointed at my plate. "Eat."

I looked back at my lasagna. Suddenly, I had no appetite at all. In fact, my stomach was doing full-blown somersaults, making me feel sick. I jumped up and grabbed my phone, dashing away despite their protests and tossing an "I'm not feeling well!" over my shoulder.

I felt *better* than well when I saw Jonah's name on the display. I practically flew up the stairs.

I rushed to the bathroom, locked the door, and sat on the toilet lid, taking a deep breath to calm myself before reading his message. *Hey, Ava. It's Jonah from D-Phi. Wyd?*

I read it over and over again, trying to think of the best way to respond. I sure as hell wasn't going to tell him I was just eating dinner with my parents—that sounded so high-school. So I finally typed in, *Hey! Not much. You?*

Immediately, three dots appeared, indicating he was replying. My breathing came in short, shallow bursts as I tapped my fingers on my thighs, waiting for him to respond.

A moment later, the message appeared: *I've just been thinking about you.*

I'd been on cloud nine before, but with that, I rocketed up into outer space, where I stayed for the entire rest of the weekend.

Chapter Seven

"Shut. The. Fuck. Up. He messaged you? When?" Penny questioned as we made our way to the cafeteria lunch line.

"Saturday, early evening," I responded with a hint of pride, happy to have proven her wrong. "And then we texted back and forth all weekend."

She pouted. "I told you to tell me the second he messaged you!"

"Sorry! I was just so busy. We seriously never stopped texting the whole time." I smiled at the memory. My fingers ached from all the texting. I'd only stopped for a couple of hours Sunday morning to get in a few hours of sleep. But when I'd woken up, I'd had another text from Jonah, and we'd texted back and forth all day long. "It was crazy."

She was silent for a moment. I'd probably surprised her; texting non-stop wasn't something the "lazy" guys, from her experience, did. But Jonah had been so nice. He'd been interested in my life, asking lots of questions. And he'd been funny and self-deprecating, too. I'd learned so much about him. I felt like we were friends. There was no way he'd be sweet to me one moment and then ditch me the next like Kyle had done to Penny.

She might have been thinking the same thing because there was a little bitterness in her tone when she said, "So... what? Are you going to see him again?"

I'd been hoping he would ask me out, but he hadn't. That was good, though. If I asked my parents if I could go out with a guy five years my senior, it'd never fly. Jonah had asked if he'd see us at another party, and I thought that was an easier workaround. "He invited us to come to another party next Saturday."

Penny collected her salad and tossed her hair. "No thanks."

She headed away, leaving my stomach churning. I grabbed my chicken nuggets, threw them on my tray and rushed to keep up with her. "What do you mean? Don't you want to see Kyle again?"

"Ugh, don't even say his name around me. I never want to see his stupid face again."

When we got to our table, Sara was already biting into her pizza. She must've heard me because she said, "There's no way we can go back there anytime soon. My parents were already suspicious after last time."

Penny gave her a look. "But you want to see Biggs again."

Sara made a face. "Maybe I would. But I gave him my number but he hasn't gotten in touch. Not like your guy, Ava. He clearly has the hots for you."

Penny nodded. "Yeah, that's why I'm pretty sure Ava's holding out on us." She fixed me with a challenging look. "Confess. You gave him a blow job. Right?"

I let out a little gasp of surprise at her directness. "*No.* We didn't do any of that. But I think he actually really likes me. I don't know why. He called me gorgeous and said he really wants to see me again."

Penny gave me a doubtful look. "Honey, it's not that you're not, but that's what they all say."

I nodded. "I know, I know. And, well, it's weird because he's so much older. Isn't it? I think he's twenty, maybe twenty-one."

"Seriously?" Sara said, a long string of pizza cheese hanging from her mouth to the plate.

"That is so hot!" Penny exclaimed. "So can he buy us all liquor so we can *really* party?"

Penny's head was always on the party. But mine was on my heart. Jonah had already written on it in the short time I'd known him. It didn't seem real that I could fall this hard and this fast, this soon. If it had happened to anyone else, I would've told them to take it slow. But here I was, eager to push on the gas and see where it took me.

"Maybe." I dipped a nugget in honey mustard absently, thinking. "I mean, he is cute, but you don't think it's weird? Like, I'm a senior in high school, and he's a senior in college. I'm sure there are plenty of other college girls that are interested in him. Why is he even talking to me?"

Penny shrugged. "You're overthinking it. Older guys are better, anyway. They're more sophisticated. You know every girl in this cafeteria is going to be so jealous of you and your college hottie."

"I don't know," Sara said, nose scrunching. "I'd proceed with caution. You just met him. He could be a serial killer, for all you know."

I gave her a look. Sara loved true crime documentaries. Her mind always seemed to spiral out in that direction.

Penny waved her off. "Babe, please."

"He'll probably lose interest when he finds out we have nothing in common," I mused. I hadn't exactly lied when I texted with him, but I'd definitely tried to sound more mature. I'd deliberately steered away from anything regarding high school or living at home with my parents.

Penny gave me a hard look. "Ava, the fact is, Jonah is into you now. He punched that guy in the face for you and he tracked you down because he likes you. I'd say keep talking to him and see what happens."

I planned to. There was no doubt in my mind. "But I'm not going to another party without you guys, and I can't have my parents find out. If he came to the door, they'd flip."

Penny laughed. "He probably won't ask you out on a date. He's a broke college kid. But if you do want to see him again, let me know. I'll cover for you."

The wheels in my mind were already turning, trying to work out our rendezvous, but I shook those thoughts away. *First things first,* I told myself. *He might not even text you again.*

But at that moment, my phone buzzed in my pocket. I fished it out and glanced at the screen. It was a text from Jonah. *Hope you're having a good day.*

And I just melted.

Chapter Eight

A horn blared outside, and my heart fluttered as I stood in my bedroom, evaluating my outfit in the full-length mirror. I'd already changed twice and carefully applied my make-up because everything had to be perfect for this, my first real date. I'd been waiting all week for this.

Actually, I'd been waiting all my *life* for this moment.

Unfortunately, it was nothing like what I'd envisioned in my fantasies—my date nervously introducing himself to my parents and standing awkwardly in the foyer while my parents peppered him with questions about his family and his career aspirations. Then, descending the staircase, only to have his eyes light up with adoration for me.

No, instead, I had Penny out in the car, driving me to the rendezvous point as if this was some kind of spy movie.

As I made my way down the stairs, I saw my parents, both at different windows, peeking out.

"I checked the schedule. The movie starts at 7:30, so you have just enough time to get a bite to eat beforehand," my mom said to me, twisting the living room curtain in her fist.

"Got it," I said, hoisting my purse onto my shoulder.

My father said, "Is Penny okay, driving all the way to the mall? That highway is a deathtrap."

I rolled my eyes. "Yeah, it's f—"

"Honey, you look so cute," my mother said, touching my sweater. "You sure got dolled up."

"Mom, please, I've got to go," I mumbled, reaching for the door.

"I'm just saying, it's nice to see you making an effort!" she said.

I glared at her. "Mom, what are you saying that I look trashy all the time?"

"No. But you don't usually wear make-up to school."

She went to hug me, but I withered under her suspicious gaze and pulled myself away. "Okay. Bye."

"Alright, have a good time and remember to be home before mid—" my mom said, but I slammed the door shut before she could finish.

When I got into the car with Penny, she was dressed as if she was going out, too. But that was nothing new. She probably was going somewhere. I smiled at her as she peeled off, tires squealing. "Thanks for doing this."

"No problem, Babe," she said. "I know you'd do it for me. If you had a car, at least."

"Are you going somewhere afterward?"

She laughed. "I can't let you have all the fun! Once I drop you off at the mall, I'm going to Kyle's. Then the plan is that Jonah will drive you back to the D-Phi house after your date, and I'll drive you back to your place. Okay?"

I just stared at her in shock. "Kyle's? But—"

"I know, I know. But when I told him about this and how you didn't want your parents to find out, he said I should hang out with him. They're not having a party or anything. Just a low-key thing."

"Oh. Cool." So we could've just gone to a party like I originally had asked if I had just pressed her? I felt like everything had changed. "What happened to you never talking to him again?"

"Oh, that. He texted me out of the blue, and he was really sweet, so I figured I'd give him another chance. Besides, nothing should stand in the way of you getting with your hot man, especially parents."

"I didn't realize. We could've gone to the party. Or you guys could've double-dated with us."

She snorted. "Who dates anymore? Except for Jonah, apparently. Trust me, we'll have plenty of fun at Kyle's place. Plus, there's nothing good playing at the Rockhill movie theater, anyway."

"Oh. Okay."

The Rockhill Mall was a decent-sized mall with a movie theater, food court, and two floors of stores. I hadn't been there in a while because it was all the same stores that catered to an older crowd, but now, fresh excitement pulsed through my veins.

We pulled up in front of the food court entrance, and I hopped out. Before I slammed the door, Penny said, "Don't have too much fun," and winked at me mischievously.

"Same to you," I said, then turned to go inside.

The court was full of the dinner crowd, but I was ten minutes early for our six o'clock date, so I assumed I'd have to wait. But the second I went in, a hand went up and waved. I stood on my toes and saw Jonah already seated at a booth.

"Hey," he said when I approached.

"Hi," I said shyly, willing my heart to stop beating like it was trying to escape my body.

A beat of awkward silence followed. My mind went absolutely blank.

Jonah scanned the different neon signs surrounding them. "So, I know this isn't some fancy dinner, but are you in the mood for pizza or Chinese, or... ?"

"Pizza," I managed.

We went up to the pizza counter, where Jonah ordered two plain slices and sodas. He paid for both of them, and we went back to the booth.

"So, everything was okay with getting here?" he asked, biting into his slice.

"Yeah... sorry. My parents..." I blushed. I'd told myself I wouldn't mention them, and it was practically the first word out of my mouth. *Nice going, Ava.*

He raised his eyebrow in such a way that made me think he'd never had parents to answer to, ever. "Oh... so you can't date?"

"It's not that." It *was* that, actually. I could probably date a guy my age, but not someone as old as Jonah. I knew my parents would never understand, and I hated how immature that made me sound. "It's just that they'd probably assault you with questions that would make the Spanish Inquisition look like child's play."

He smiled, and a rush of pleasure coursed through my body over having said something witty, something that had clearly impressed him. "Hey. I don't mind parents. I have them too, you know. Next time, I can pick you up at your house."

Next time. My heart skipped. "Well, it's not just that. It's... well, I'm seventeen. And you're..."

"Ah, got it." He nodded with understanding, then stroked his chin, thinking. "Hmm."

It seemed insurmountable, but if there was going to be a next time and a time after that, I couldn't keep sneaking around and using Penny as my alibi. "I hate lying, but I don't know what else to do."

He frowned repulsed, which made me like him more. "No. Don't do that." He held up a finger. "Here's what you do. Invite me over for dinner. By the end of it, I guarantee your parents will love me."

I blinked. Didn't guys usually sweat over meeting the girl's parents? It had never occurred to me that he'd welcome the chance. I'd never met anyone so self-assured before. And if he met my parents at a real dinner, wasn't that a big step from "hanging out" to "relationship"? My heart quivered in my chest. "Are you sure?"

"Absolutely," he said before taking a gulp of his Coke. "You have siblings?"

Since I'd just taken a bite of my pizza, I shook my head, trying not to look like an idiot with cheese dripping down my chin.

"Spoiled only child, huh?" Before I could decide whether to be offended, he smiled. "Me too."

Funny, despite the age difference, he made it seem like we had so much in common. We talked some more, and I was surprised at how easy it was and how my nervousness disappeared.

Maybe it was because Jonah had already had it in his head that we would have a next date. And as I talked, I never felt like someone was as interested in something I had to say more than Jonah was at that moment. It made my heart tighten as I gazed into his warm brown eyes.

After we finished eating, we headed over to the movie theater, where Jonah bought both our tickets and a large popcorn to share. When we found our theater, the lights were already dimmed since the coming attractions had started. Jonah led the way through the dark theater to seats in the back row.

After we sat down, Jonah leaned in and said, "I love sitting in the back row. You aren't too close to the screen, and you get your privacy because no one can sit behind you."

I suppressed a nervous giggle and reached for the popcorn, thinking, *Why do we need privacy? Just what does he have in mind?*

The movie was some star-studded rom-com, and we quieted down to watch. I liked the way my hand sometimes bumped into Jonah's if we both reached for popcorn at the same time.

At first, I really couldn't focus on the movie. I kept wanting to look over at Jonah to see if he was enjoying the movie... and, more importantly, my company. But eventually, when the plot started to thicken, and the popcorn ran out, I became absorbed in the movie.

It was just then that I felt a warm hand wrap around mine.

I looked down at my lap and noticed Jonah had interlaced his fingers with mine. His hand was warm and perfect. I looked over at him and smiled, but his eyes were fastened on the screen. He was so casual about holding my hand that I suddenly felt younger than seventeen. Jonah was older and had probably held hands with other girls before, but this was my first time holding hands with a boy.

No, a man.

And I liked it so much that I barely noticed when the movie ended. It was only when the lights came up, and he loosened his grip and looked at me, that I woke up from the dream world he'd cast me into.

As he walked me to the car, he stayed close to me so I could smell his cologne mixed with the buttery goodness of the popcorn. His cologne was fresh, almost minty, and it made me want to give him a hug so I could breathe in more of that smell.

When we reached a beat-up silver Audi, one of the few cars left in the lot, Jonah jogged a little bit ahead of me and opened the passenger side door to let me in. "Good?" he asked, handing me the seatbelt.

I nodded.

He's so gentlemanly, I thought as he jogged to the driver's side. *He didn't even try anything at all in the movie theater.*

Jonah started the engine, and loud rock music blared through the speakers as he made his way onto the road.

"You know, no one has ever opened the car door for me before. That was really sweet of you," I said.

As if he could read my mind, he said, "Oh, it's nothing. I know chivalry is dying, but I like to think of myself as a gentleman. I guess you'll be the judge of that."

As we made our way back to the Icana campus, a knot began to grow in my stomach. How would this date end? Not with a handshake. He'd want a kiss.

Maybe I could do that.

No, *of course,* I could do that. Yes, Jonah had probably kissed a thousand girls before in his many more years on this Earth. He was probably a good kisser. But I could be one, too, with enough practice. Maybe it was like dancing, and a good partner was all it took.

I ran my tongue around my teeth, wondering if my breath was okay. Wondering if he'd try it in the car or when we got out. Wondering if I'd do something that would appall him, like have too much saliva in my mouth and make him never want to talk to me again.

I was still in my head thinking about the worst-case scenario when I realized the car had stopped, and we were sitting in front of the fraternity house.

"Ava, are you okay?" Jonah asked as he turned off the engine.

"Yeah. I'm fine."

"Just wanted to make sure because you barely talked the whole way home."

"I'm just a little tired, that's all. I had a really great time, though!"

"I had a good time, too. Let's go find Penny."

We got out of the car and made our way through the parking lot, stopping on the porch that had been filled last time with drunken party-goers and a keg. It brought back all the memories of our first meeting. As he reached for the door, a burly guy in a D-

Phi sweatshirt was coming out.

"Hey, Jonah. You're on pledge duty tonight."

Jonah rolled his eyes. "Yeah. You seen Kyle?"

The guy gave a short laugh and said, "In his room. But he has company."

"I'm here," a guy said, appearing at the top of the steps in nothing but boxers, his thick, dark hair standing up on his head. If that was Kyle, he was kind of short and pudgy, especially in the middle. I couldn't see what Penny saw in him. He winked at me and dragged Penny into sight. "Your ride is here."

"Bye, Kyle!" Penny, fully dressed but with her make-up smeared and hair wild, came bounding down the stairs, grinning. "How did you guys do?"

"Good," I said lamely, but Jonah said, "It was a fantastic night," which made me feel warm all over.

"Well, I'll wait in the car and let you say goodnight," she said, tottering down the stairs in her high heels. Kyle had already disappeared; the asshole couldn't even bother to get dressed to walk her to her car.

With that, Jonah and I were left alone. I watched Penny step around the house toward the lot and disappear from sight, thinking about how some guys could be such scumbags. Some guys. But not this one. Not Jonah. He was a saint. "By the way, I never thanked you for stopping that guy at the party."

He tilted his head. "What are you talking about?"

"That guy that grabbed me and was dancing on me at the party. You punched him and told him to get away from me."

He hesitated at the door and looked down at me with a small smile on his face. "Oh right, right. That was nothing."

I smiled at his chivalry. He was like a knight in shining armor. Willing to come to anyone's aid, but so humble about it. "It was something."

"Ava, I would do anything to keep you safe," he said softly, lowering his lips to mine. The kiss only lasted a few seconds, not even long enough for me to register what was happening. By the time I realized that I was being kissed by Jonah Manzano, he was already pulling away.

It left me absolutely speechless.

He pushed a lock of hair out of my eyes, behind my ear, so gently, as if I was something precious. Then he said, "I'll text you tomorrow. Have a good night, Ava."

I felt Jonah's kiss lingering on my lips as I watched him go inside. I was not only speechless, I was completely in love.

Chapter Nine

"He kissed you! Oh my god! How was it?" Sara yelled over the phone.

I'd woke up the next morning to a text from my friend's group chat—Penny spilling the beans over all the details I'd given her on the ride home. Since Jonah had quickly become my favorite topic of conversation, I couldn't wait until after breakfast to have this conversation.

"Yes! He walked me to the door and kissed me. It was quick but absolutely wonderful. Jonah was such a gentleman."

"He's so cute. I'm so jealous! Ava's going to have a boyfriend and forget about us all," said Sara, sounding wistful.

"No, she won't. She'll ask Jonah to get us alcohol so we can party anytime we want," Penny laughed. "Or she'd better if she doesn't want us to be her *ex*-best friends."

"I thought you already had Kyle for that!" Sara said.

She snorted. "Kyle's only nineteen."

"Oh," Sara said. "Speaking of Kyle... How was that?"

"Oh, good. Really good," Penny said, which was all she'd told me on the ride home. I wasn't sure why she was being so mysterious since I wanted to talk about every detail of my kiss with Jonah. But that was Penny—she liked to tell just enough to keep us guessing. "I think he might be inviting us all to another party soon. It's a huge homecoming blow-out."

"Sounds cool," Sara said. "Did you see Biggs there?"

"No, why? Have you been talking?"

"Yeah... well, no. Not lately. He's all hot and heavy one minute, and then he just up and ghosts me the next. I haven't heard boo from him in three days."

While they were going on, my phone buzzed with a text. I pulled it away from my ear and saw Jonah's name, which made my body tingle all over.

"Ava, why aren't you saying anything?" asked Penny.

I blinked out of my love trance when I heard my name. "Oh, sorry. Jonah just texted me."

"Ohhhh, what did he say?"

"He said, 'Good morning, beautiful.'"

The girls squealed with excitement, and I joined in.

"I've got to say," Penny said, her voice low. "That guy is smooth."

I wasn't sure what she meant by that. Was she saying it was just a line? That he'd said the same to hundreds of girls?

Maybe. Possibly. But I didn't want to think about that. Besides, he'd seemed so sincere with me. Though it hadn't started out as the fantasy I'd imagined, it had been the perfect first date. "I don't know. He's such a gentleman. You should've seen him opening the doors for me. I felt like a princess."

Penny let out a sarcastic snort.

I was surprised at how much that one sound could hurt me. "What's that supposed to mean, Pen?"

"It's because he wants some," she said in a sing-song voice. "Trust me."

"*No*," I was quick to say. "He didn't even try anything in the movie theater. He just held my hand."

Penny said, "Mmmhmmm, if you say so," as if she knew so much better. And maybe she did. But not all guys were like Kyle. Maybe the ones she attracted were. But I refused to believe that her blanket statement applied to every guy on Earth.

I sighed. This conversation was bringing me down. I couldn't wait until we were past this stage where everyone was questioning

Jonah's motives. We'd prove them wrong. We just had to wait it out. "I've got to go."

Once I hung up with my friends, I heard my phone buzz. It was Jonah again. *Last night was perfect, and I can't wait to see you again.*

I beamed from ear to ear. It was like he'd read my mind. Then I typed in, *When do you want to meet up?*

I waited on the edge of my bed, feeling so relaxed, soaking in the warm sunshine streaming through the blinds. But when I read his next message: *That depends on when your parents want to have me,* my spine stiffened.

Right. I had to tell my parents and hope they wouldn't kill me or demand I never see Jonah again.

Neither of those options would work for me.

I went downstairs to find my parents at the kitchen table. They'd eaten breakfast already, but my father was working on a crossword puzzle, and my mother was watching the morning show on the television. She stood up in her robe as I came in. "Morning, Honey! Want breakfast? It's pancakes and bacon!"

"Sure," I said, but not because I was hungry. I didn't think I could eat anything, as nervous as I was.

"Hey, pumpkin," my father said, clearing a space at the table for me. "Have fun last night?"

I nodded. "Um... guys..." I took a deep breath. "If I wanted to invite a guest over for dinner one night next week, would you let me?"

My mother turned away from the stove and looked at me. "Of course, you've had Sara and Penny here before..." Her eyes lit up. "Do you mean a boy?"

I nodded. "Well, he's—"

She turned off the stove and came close to me. "Oh. Who is he? Is he from Woodrow Wilson? How long have you been boyfriend and girlfriend? Have you—"

"Mom!" I said, holding out my hands. "Wait. I just met him. I've hung out with him in a group thing, when I was with Penny."

It wasn't a *total* lie.

She nodded. "Oh. He doesn't go to school with you?"

"No, he—"

"So he's a friend of Penny's? Because even so, we'd want to meet him first before you went out. Just to be safe," she said, looking at my father, who nodded in agreement. "He should come to dinner. Does he go to Catholic?"

I gritted my teeth. "Not exactly."

My father looked up from his crossword. "Not exactly? Does he go to that private all-boys high school in—"

"He doesn't go to high school at all. He's in college at Icana."

They looked at one another, then back at me. My mother said, "An *older* boy? Oh. Well, I suppose that's all right. Your father's a year older than me."

I winced. "He's a senior," I said, my voice small.

My father's eyes went wide. "Ava... do you think that's a good idea?"

"That's why I wanted you to meet him first," I blurted, looking down. Somehow, I'd torn my napkin to shreds. "He's pretty nice, I think. But if you think it's a problem, I won't go out with him."

They looked at one another, having a silent conversation with their eyes. Then my mother said, "How about this Thursday? And see if he likes roast beef."

I said a silent prayer of thanks in my head as I nodded. "Great! I will. Thanks, guys."

As my mother put on the pancakes, I grabbed my phone, eager to tell him the news. Everything was going to be okay. I could just feel it.

Chapter Ten

The week flew by, with me on top of the world. Jonah texted me nonstop the whole time. He told me constantly how beautiful I was and how much he liked kissing me. He told me how much he enjoyed our time together. He asked how my day was going, and if I was a little down about something, he'd send a stupid joke to cheer me up. Thursday afternoon, I couldn't stop smiling as my friends and I walked out of the front doors of Wood Wil.

"Jonah is picking you up today, right?" Penny asked me.

"Yep. My mom is making dinner for us."

"That's so nice! Meeting the parents is a big step. I can't believe he let you sucker him into it after just one date."

"He's the one who suggested it," I said, proud of how mature Jonah was.

"He must really want it bad," Penny said with a laugh.

I glared at her. Why did she always think about sex? There were some people who liked to get to know each other first. Not every guy was a massive horndog like Kyle.

"It'll be fine. Jonah sounds like a sweetheart," Sara piped up, smiling at me. "Plus, Ava is basically in love with him, so her parents will probably like him too. You have nothing to worry about."

I smiled, suddenly embarrassed. Was it that obvious? Yes, I guess I had been talking about Jonah a lot. I couldn't help it. He was so easy to think about, to gush about. It was pretty obvious that he had me wrapped around his finger.

I was still grinning as I separated from my friends and made my way to the parent pick-up parking lot. I looked around for Jonah's silver sedan but couldn't quite remember what it looked like. It was such a generic car, and I wasn't a car person.

After wandering about aimlessly, looking into the driver's seats of all the silver cars I could see, I decided to text Jonah and let him know where I was. *I'm here in the lot. Are you here?*

After doing another lap on the sidewalk in front of the lot, I was pretty sure the answer was no. Not that he'd texted me back. I had told him yesterday that I got out of school at 3:30 pm, hadn't I? That wasn't my imagination. He'd said he'd be there waiting.

So where was he?

The lot continued to clear out until it was practically empty. I kept checking my phone. It was 3:45 now, and the marching band and football team were starting to filter out onto the field to practice. I felt like a fool standing there as they all walked past me.

Maybe he's in the wrong lot, I thought, walking toward the front lot, where the students parked.

I stood on the sidewalk and watched the last of the students climbing into their cars and pulling away. I watched until there was only one car left—a red Jeep. Definitely not Jonah's. *Our wires must've gotten crossed. He's probably waiting for me in the wrong place.*

I checked my phone again. *Then why hasn't he texted or called?*

I dialed his number, but it went straight to voicemail.

So I did the only thing I could do. I sat on the curb, watching as the last cars pulled out of the lot. I saw some teachers I knew but pretended I didn't notice them. It was chilly, so I shivered in my thin sweater since I'd forgotten to bring a coat. It was a little embarrassing since most kids flew out of the high school as if escaping a prison, to still be there after I'd been set free.

Then I called his number again, feeling terrible. I'd said Wood Wil, but maybe I hadn't given him clear enough directions. Maybe he'd gone to a different school.

And now my mom was probably at home, getting the roast beef all prepared for a special meal. I'd probably have to call her and tell her to forget it.

Also, I'd need a ride home. How embarrassing was that? My first boyfriend, and here I was, stood up. Maybe he'd thought twice about meeting the parents and wasn't ready for that, just like Penny said. It was a big step.

My mind continued to spiral until another thought occurred to me. *Or, god, maybe he's been in an accident?*

After that, I really started to worry. I checked the time again. 4:05 pm. Seriously, Jonah was too considerate. He wouldn't be that late, would he?

Just when I was about to call my mother, I saw a small silver car pull into the parking lot entrance. The car drove right up to the sidewalk where I was sitting, shivering. Jonah got out of the car and walked over to the passenger's side to open the door for me.

He looked surprisingly disheveled in his gray sweatpants and wrinkled t-shirt, but his charm had not left him. "Hey, beautiful."

"You're late," I said, standing up and trying to keep my tone as playful as possible despite my chattering teeth.

"Oh, am I?" Jonah pulled out his phone to check the time. "I didn't realize."

"You didn't see my texts or call?"

"No. Actually, I think my phone was on silent, but I'm here now, so are you ready to go?" There was a little bit of bite in his voice.

Okay, so he's not going to apologize?

He could have at least had an excuse. I wanted to tell him that I was disappointed, but I didn't want to ruin the evening by having our first argument now. So, I climbed into the car without another word.

When we got to my house, I took a deep breath as I opened the door. Time to introduce Jonah to the family. Glancing back at him, I couldn't help but scrutinize his wardrobe. It was like he hadn't even made an effort. I expected he'd wear nice jeans and a sweater or something, not that he'd look like he just came from the gym. Hadn't he said he'd work really hard to win them over?

No, actually, he hadn't said he'd work hard. He'd just said he'd win them over. Maybe he was one of those people who managed to make everyone fall for him without doing a thing.

But that's not going to work. My parents aren't so easily swayed.

Biting my lip, I opened the door, and we were greeted with the savory aroma of my mom's roast beef.

"Something smells really good in here!" Jonah said as we walked into the kitchen.

"Oh! I didn't hear you kids come in. Thank you! So, this must be Jonah!" she said, giving him an embarrassingly obvious inspection like he's a piece of fruit in the produce aisle of the supermarket.

He extended his hand for her to shake. "Nice to meet you, Mrs. Parker."

"Nice to meet you! How was school, honey?" Mrs. Parker asked.

Okay, so far, so good. "It was good. Penny and I are partners on this history assignment."

"That's nice. Dinner should be ready in about fifteen minutes if you want to make yourselves at home. Or you could give Jonah a little tour of the house."

Having survived the introductions to my mom, my mind switched to the next obstacle. "Sure. Where's Dad?"

"In the backyard, I think. He'll be in in a moment."

I showed Jonah where to hang up his coat and take off his shoes before we made our way around the house, starting with the living room and continuing on to the dining room, which was set up with good china and silverware. That was a rare sight. We usually only ate at the dining room table on holidays. At least my mom was trying to put her best foot forward to impress Jonah.

Once we finished exploring the first floor, I led Jonah upstairs and showed him my bedroom. I'd always loved my bedroom, but the moment I opened the door, I cringed with embarrassment over the ruffled pink bedspread and animal posters on the walls.

"Wow, so this is where the beautiful Miss Ava sleeps?" Jonah asked as he plopped down on my bed and sprawled out.

"It sure is. And this is where I do my makeup in the morning," I said, motioning to my vanity.

Jonah stood up and came close to me. "A waste of space, if you ask me. You have so much natural beauty; you don't need to wear makeup."

I blushed, buoyed by those words. It was crazy that I could have such strong feelings for a guy I'd only known for a few weeks. But after years of walking the halls of Wood Wil, feeling practically invisible, Jonah made me feel so beautiful and seen. I didn't want this feeling to ever go away.

"Come here," he whispered, and I obeyed. He wrapped me into his arms and really kissed me. This time, his tongue slipped between my mouth and nibbled on my lips, letting out a little moan that told me he was enjoying it. I was intoxicated by the feeling of his lips on mine and by the light scent of his cologne. "God, you taste so good," he said as if he was under the same spell.

I barely noticed when he shuffled me across the room and pulled me onto the bed on top of him. I was so lost in the feeling of his strong arms around me and the way he kissed me. I wanted it to go on forever. That is until sanity intervened, and I remembered where I was.

My mom could walk in on us at any moment!

I pulled away, glancing at the door as I tried to wiggle out of Jonah's embrace. "We really shouldn't. Not here, not now."

"Why not here?" he said with a mischievous grin. "No time like the present."

"Because my parents are right downstairs," I whispered, combing a hand through my mussed hair.

"I can't wait to really show you how much I like you, Ava," Jonah said as he leaned in to kiss me again. I wanted to, and I was excited to find out just what he meant, but I was also nervous about entering this strange new world. I trusted Jonah, but I couldn't stop thinking of my parents.

"We should probably head back downstairs. I'm sure dinner will be ready soon," I said as I stood up.

"Yeah, okay. Let's go eat." He sounded a little annoyed, which worried me. I didn't want him meeting my father when he wasn't in the right mood to be charming.

"Are you okay?" I asked him, reaching for his hand playfully.

He let me take it, but he didn't grip mine. "Yeah, fine. Let's go."

My heart caught. I hoped Penny wasn't right. After all the time I'd spent telling them what a gentleman he was, I didn't want to think that he was doing this all because he wanted me to give it up. That couldn't have been it, I reassured myself. If all he wanted was sex, he could've gotten that from any number of girls on campus. It sure would've been a lot easier than going through meeting my parents.

When we went into the dining room, my mother was placing

the carved roast beef at the center of the table, along with roasted vegetables and homemade mashed potatoes, my favorite. "You can sit here," I told him, pointing to the chair across from me.

As we were sitting down, my father came in. "Wow, this smells amazing, hon!" he exclaimed as he gave my mom a kiss. "Ah, you must be Jonah."

He extended his hand, and Jonah reached out to shake it. "Yes, sir."

"We're glad to have you here, Jonah. Ava has told us a lot about you. Icana University, huh?"

"Thank you for inviting me. Yes, sir. I really enjoy spending time with Ava." Jonah gave me a small smile.

We passed around the serving dishes and dug in, conversing. The whole time, Jonah was polite and well-spoken. He sounded serious and ambitious, talking about his future. He explained about his business, buying things wholesale and selling them on Amazon and eBay. He also told them things I didn't know, like how he'd lived with his parents while commuting to school until moving into the fraternity house last semester to finish up his senior year. The anxiety I'd felt melted away as I watched him, clearly in his element. I could tell my parents were impressed.

It's like he's part of the family already!

As my parents cleared the plates off the table and went into the kitchen to grab dessert, I whispered, "I think you are winning them over."

"Of course," he said as if he'd never had a doubt, reaching for my hand across the table. "I'm having such a great time. I'm so glad you invited me over."

"I am, too."

We leaned toward each other, grinning as if we were the only people in the world.

He whispered in my ear, "Hey. Why don't we watch a movie after dessert? I don't want to go home just yet."

I would've liked nothing more, but I'd been so nervous about this meeting that I'd completely spaced on Chemistry. And tomorrow was our big test. I needed to play catch-up if I was going to pass it.

"I actually have some homework to get done, but we can definitely hang out this weekend?"

Jonah's smile faded as he dropped my hand. It was like a shadow crept over his face, the same one I'd seen upstairs when I told him I didn't want to fool around with my parents so close by. "Yeah, maybe. I don't know. I have an internship interview to prepare for."

My stomach plummeted. It was shocking how his face and features could turn to stone so quickly before my eyes. He wouldn't look at me. I hadn't expected that one sentence would ruin everything. But what could I do?

Luckily, my mom walked through the doorway, breaking the icy silence lingering between us.

"Coconut cream pie from Robert's Farm," she sang as she placed the pie on the table, my father following behind with a knife and dessert plates.

"Really?" I asked, impressed. They were going all out. Robert's Farm was a family favorite. Each pie was more delicious than the next, no matter the flavor, but it was usually something we only got on holidays.

The conversation picked right back up, and I breathed out a sigh of relief when Jonah continued contributing just as easily as he had during dinner. My parents did like him, which was good, because I wanted there to be a next time, and to have their blessing. I hoped I hadn't ruined things with him. Maybe it would blow over.

I just needed to learn how to be a bit more flexible when it came to making plans, so I wouldn't let him down.

When the conversation died down, and the dessert plates were empty, Jonah stood up.

"Alright, well, I better be going. I know Ava has a lot of homework to get done, and I don't want to take time away from that," he said, shaking hands with my parents again.

"We'd love to have you again," my mother said. "Be careful on the way home."

I stood up, too. "Let me grab my coat, and I'll walk you out."

Outside, I gave Jonah a big hug as we stood in front of his car. Was it my imagination, or was he not wrapping his arms around me as tightly as he had before?

"I think my parents liked you," I said, hoping that would lighten the mood.

"You think?"

"Yeah! My parents aren't usually that talkative."

He didn't seem as happy as I'd hoped and wouldn't meet my eyes. "Mhhhm."

A sick sensation sunk into my gut. Why did I suddenly feel like he might ghost me as Biggs had done to Sara? "So, this weekend then?"

Jonah took a step back and ran a hand through his hair. "Yeah. I'll let you know."

That sounded noncommittal, lacking the energy and excitement he'd had before. My heart twisted as he leaned down to give me a quick kiss. It wasn't like the kisses he'd given me earlier; it was like something he'd give his grandmother.

As he got into the car, I wanted to say something, do something to make it all right. I silently cursed my chemistry teacher. Chemistry was ridiculous, anyway. Who cared if I failed the test?

I had a B-plus in that class, anyway. One test wouldn't matter.

"Wait—" I began, but he'd already slammed the car door and started the engine.

I watched him drive off, wondering why he'd gotten so disappointed. He had classes, too. He had to know that it was important to do well. He shouldn't have gotten so upset. And yet, I couldn't help feeling it was my fault and my problem to fix.

Studying chemistry didn't really happen, either. I couldn't concentrate on covalent bonding. I kept replaying my conversation with him and wondering how I could've fixed things. I checked my phone as I got ready for bed, feeling more and more desperate as the minutes ticked by. No messages from Jonah. He had to have been home by now. Was this it? Was this the end?

No, it couldn't be. I thought about how my parents had fallen in love with him, and how my friends were so jealous, how everything seemed to be going so well. Not to mention, he was sweet, chivalrous, smart, and fun. He was everything.

I couldn't just let this go. I had to do something. So, before I went to bed, I texted him:

I had a really good time tonight, and I'm sorry for upsetting you. I really didn't want you to go. Good night.

I didn't sleep at all that night. I kept checking my phone every ten minutes to see if he'd texted. But he never did.

Chapter Eleven

A few days went by before Jonah texted me again.

Excruciating days. At lunch the Friday after our big dinner with the parents, I told my friends it had been great and that my parents seemed to approve of our relationship. But that night, I tossed and turned in bed without a word from Jonah, thinking, *What relationship?*

It felt like it was over even before it had really begun. What a waste.

The weekend had been horrible and lonely, with me checking my phone constantly, wondering if he was even thinking about me at all. It felt like I was being punished simply for having a life outside him. Then I felt like an idiot because *he* probably had a life outside *me*, and that was why he wasn't calling. I should've been like him instead of obsessing over him.

But then he went and texted me so casually on Monday afternoon as nothing had happened: *Hey, what's up?*

After that, we texted like normal. I didn't want to bring up our little fight because he had clearly forgotten it. We texted like crazy for the rest of the week, and he kept saying how much he missed me and wanted to see me again. But he never proposed any plans. So, on Friday afternoon, I still had no idea what I was doing that weekend.

I met up with Penny and Sara when school let out, and we walked to the parking lot.

"Is Jonah taking you out tonight?" Penny asked.

"No. I don't know when I'm seeing him again." I fsrowned at the floor.

"What? What do you mean you don't know when you're

seeing him next? I thought he wanted to see you like every day.”

“Yeah, well, he’s busy. He’s been preparing for an internship interview,” I said, which wasn’t a lie. At least, I didn’t think it was. It was clearly important to him since he’d mentioned it a few times. It was in Pittsburgh for some start-up, and he needed it to graduate.

Penny snorted doubtfully. “Ava, listen. You cannot mess this up! College boys don’t come knocking on high school girls’ doors that often.”

Penny was right. I was lucky to have Jonah interested in me. He had so much to offer, and what did I have? I was still in high school, didn’t have a job, didn’t have a car... didn’t have anything. Well, except for a curfew.

“He’s still texting you, right?” Sara chimed in.

“Yeah.”

“Okay, then he’s still into you,” Sara reassured me.

“But he’ll lose interest if she doesn’t make some big moves soon,” Penny said.

I looked at her, hoping she wasn’t meaning what I thought she meant. Penny had slept with Kyle, but it didn’t seem to be helping her. “How are things with you and Kyle?” I asked casually.

She made a sick face. “As a matter of fact, I never want to see Kyle again... but if he happened to see me with an even cuter college guy, I wouldn’t object, so see if Jonah will invite us to the next D-Phi party.” She winked.

Judging from that, I gathered that Kyle hadn’t gotten in touch with her since last weekend. “What’s going on?”

She shrugged. “He’s just getting on my nerves. Men. You know? Can’t live with them... can’t run over them multiple times with your car.”

We all burst out laughing.

“You know what? Let’s forget guys, for tonight and have a

girl's night. I'm pretty sure the football team has a home game tonight. Let's go! We used to go like every week last year and it was so much fun," Sara said.

"Ugh, I'm kind of over the large crowds of screaming fans, but I'll go," said Penny.

"Yeah, okay. Sounds like fun," I said, smiling.

When I got home, I was excited to hang out with my friends since I hadn't spent a lot of time with them outside of school that year. Sara was right. We used to have a blast at the football games last year, splitting a giant boat of fries and getting huge blue raspberry slushies. Besides, I couldn't let Jonah occupy too much of my thoughts. I had to have a life outside him. This would be a great way to get Jonah off my mind.

But I was just pulling on a new pair of jeans and trying to think of where I'd left my hand warmers, in case it got cold when I heard the distant sound of the doorbell and my mom calling me from downstairs.

As I got to the top of the staircase, I saw Jonah looking up at me, holding a big bouquet of daisies.

My jaw dropped to the floor and I'm not sure how I made it down the stairs, but I must've been floating on air.

When I was standing on the bottom step, Jonah leaned in to give me a long, slow kiss. I didn't even care that my mother was probably nearby. I got so lost in it, his scent, his presence. I suddenly didn't care about football games, or friends, or anything. It felt like we were the only two people on Earth.

"Hi Ava, these are for you," he said when we finally parted, handing the bouquet to me with a hint of mischief in his eyes.

I took in their scent with a deep breath. "They're beautiful."

I stood there for a moment, smiling at him, just in awe that he was here and that he'd thought to give me flowers! How many men did that for their significant others? Especially young men. In that moment, all the doubt and worries I'd had about him ghosting me seemed to evaporate. He cared about me. I had to be the luckiest girl in the world.

Then Jonah said, "So, I know you probably ate already, but do you want to watch a movie or go grab ice cream or something?"

"Yeah! I mean…yeah, I'd like to, but I was actually heading out in a few minutes…" I trailed off when I saw Jonah's face fall. I didn't want to upset him again, especially since he'd been so sweet with the flowers. I wanted to spend time with him, but I couldn't cancel on the girls.

"Oh? I didn't realize you had plans," he muttered, taking a seat on the steps.

"Yeah, I'm just meeting Sara and Penny at the football game," I said quickly so he wouldn't think I was dating some other guy. That gave me an idea. "You know what, you should totally come with me! I'd love for you to formally meet Sara and Penny, and I don't think they'd mind if you tagged along."

But his face didn't change. "I don't know, Ava. I don't really want to crash your night out with your friends. It's just a shame because I did drive all this way to come see you."

It was a shame. Instantly, I felt terrible. He'd given me flowers, and this was how I treated him?

"I know, but I didn't know when I was seeing you this weekend…but it's totally fine. You can just come with us…" I trailed off again as Jonah put his head in his hands. "What is it? Do you not want to go to the football game?"

"It's just that I put a lot of effort into surprising you tonight. I couldn't stop thinking about what flowers to get you. I wanted them to be perfect. I wanted you to have the best bouquet in the shop. I even called ahead to have them specially made for you. I thought you'd like the surprise and be happy to see me. And now it feels like you're trying to get rid of me. I guess it was a pretty stupid idea, my coming over here tonight, huh?"

I hadn't thought of it like that. Jonah was right. He did pick an amazing bouquet of flowers, and had to have put in a lot of effort. I was being selfish.

"No, no I really do appreciate it, Jonah. I was so happy to see you tonight. It's fine. I'll just let Penny and Sara know I can't make it, and we can watch a movie. Like you wanted to." I smiled.

"If that's what you want to do," he said with a shrug as if it was my idea all along.

"I came here to see you, so that works." He picked himself off the stairs and kissed me again.

I could hear my parents in the kitchen, so I told Jonah to make himself comfortable and figure out what to watch while I got the flowers some water and popped popcorn.

"Hey, guys, is it okay if Jonah and I use the family room to watch a movie?" I asked as I put the flowers in the sink and reached for a vase.

"Well, I don't know, Ava," my mother said, glancing at my dad. "We were just going to go out to dinner ourselves. I don't know if it's right to leave you two alone."

"Mom!" I groaned, lacing my hands together to beg. "It's totally fine! I'm seventeen! And it's not like we're going out to a wild party. We're just staying in and watching a movie."

My mother said, "I thought you were going out with the girls?"

"Change of plans," I said, avoiding her concerned gaze. "I can't just abandon Jonah after he did all this for me."

My father grinned. "Flowers have that effect on women."

My mom smacked his shoulder lightly. "If it's that easy to impress us, then I wonder why you don't get them for me more often?" she teased.

"I think it's fine," my father said to me, probably to avoid the subject. "We're only going to be a couple of hours anyway."

Good old Dad. I sighed with relief as my mom helped me arrange the flowers in the vase. "They're beautiful, honey. He's certainly very thoughtful. Have a good time tonight."

I put the vase on a windowsill, snapped a photo, and quickly sent it to the girls: *Jonah came over and surprised me with this tonight, so I can't make it. Raincheck, ok?*

Sara responded with a sad emoji and then, *Beautiful flowers, tho!*

Penny didn't respond right away, which was odd for her. But then she said: *You lucky bitch,* with a winking emoji.

My parents gave me kisses and headed out. Closing the door behind them, I walked into the living room, still smiling at my phone, and placed the popcorn on the coffee table.

"What are you smiling about?" Jonah asked.

"My friends are jealous that I'm dating the sweetest guy ever," I said with a shrug. "I sent them a picture of the flowers."

He seemed to get a kick out of that. "Oh, they think I'm sweet, huh? How about you? Do you think I'm sweet?"

I sat down close to him and said, "I think you're the sweetest, most thoughtful, and amazing guy. My friends should be very jealous."

Jonah seemed satisfied with that answer because he put his arm around my shoulder and pulled me even closer so that I was flush against him.

"So, your parents are gone, huh?" He had a mischievous look in his eye.

I nodded. "They went out to dinner, but they won't be gone long."

I waited for him to explain just what he had in that mind of his since it was clear the gears in his head were turning. But instead, he just thrust his chin at the screen of our television.

"I think I found a couple of good ones," he said, scrolling through the choices until he landed on a new thriller that had just come out. "This one's supposed to be excellent..."

"That one sounds good. I wanted to see it in the theater."

"Cool." He turned it on, and I started to settle down next to him.

"Do you think you could grab a blanket?" he asked as I reached for the popcorn.

"Sure." I grabbed an old afghan my grandmother had knitted, and he draped it over both of us, pulling me close so I could lean against his chest. He put the popcorn bowl on his lap so that we could share.

A few minutes into the movie, Jonah set the empty popcorn bowl down on the table and started running his hand up and down my arm. It felt warm and inviting, but it also made shivers climb up the back of my neck. We were alone now for *hours*.

Suddenly I felt like I was being dragged down beneath the waves, and they soon would be over my head.

I swallowed the lump forming in my throat. "Do you want me to make more popcorn?"

"No, I just want you," Jonah said before pressing his mouth against mine.

I was a little startled by the sudden kiss, but I kissed back anyway. I could still hear the movie playing in the background, but I didn't care anymore. It felt so right to kiss Jonah.

Stop worrying, Ava. Just relax and let it happen.

His hands moved under the blanket to my hips, and he easily slid my body on top of his as he laid back on the couch. The transition was so smooth it made me wonder how many times Jonah had done this before, how many girls he'd made out with, and if he'd gone even further than that.

Of course, he has. Jonah is 21. And he's hot. He's probably hooked up with a lot of other girls before.

The thought made my stomach squirm, even before Jonah ran his hands up and down the sides of my waist, fingers flirting with the bottom of my bra. He deepened the kiss, expertly teasing my mouth with his tongue while his hands softly cupped my breasts outside my bra.

A sensation I'd never felt before coursed through me. As scared as I was, a deeper part of me, one that had just awakened, wanted more.

He continued to kiss me, gently squeezing my breasts before moving his hands around to my back. In one easy movement, I felt the clasp come undone.

He definitely has done this before.

Then he pulled back, breath ragged, and started to pull my sweater up over my head. I stiffened. "Wait..."

He stopped. "What's wrong?"

"Well, I..."

He smiled. "Ava, I told you I wanted to show you how much you mean to me. You're my girlfriend now. I told all the guys about you. That I'm with the hottest girl in Seagreen, they're all jealous."

I blinked. *Girlfriend?* I wasn't just a girl he was hooking up with. I was his girlfriend.

"Come on, Ava," he said, gazing at my breasts hungrily, tugging the bottom hem of my sweater again. "You're so hot. I've got to see you."

The way he was looking at me, I almost believed it. But he had never seen me naked. He had never even seen me without a sweater or jacket on. Maybe I was too pudgy for him, or my boobs weren't big enough.

But I was his girlfriend. And I'd loved that feeling of wanting more of giving into these new sensations and just letting my body do what felt right. So, I let him pull the sweater off my head and shrugged the bra off, then hugged myself, nerves rippling with self-consciousness over offering myself up for his approval.

And all that worry melted away when Jonah leaned in and put his mouth around one of my nipples, only to be replaced by a different one. It felt weird. As much as I wanted to like it, instead, I started to freak out. Jonah was obviously more experienced than me. That much was clear by the way he sucked and licked on my breasts.

Here I was, in my parents' family room, the room I'd watched countless Disney movies with my family, half-naked and straddling a guy while he sucked on my nipples.

Just relax, Ava. You can't tell him no. He gets so upset when you tell him no.

I closed my eyes, trying to block that out, but it was even worse. I saw myself as if peeking through the front window, and then I saw my parents' shocked faces if they found out just what I was up to.

I froze. This was too much, too fast.

As he started to kiss his way back up to my neck, I groped around the couch for my sweater.

He stopped and looked into my eyes. "Is everything okay?"

"Yeah, I... I'm just a little cold." I glanced around for my sweater but didn't see it anywhere. "Do you think we can just go back to kissing?"

"Um, yeah, sure. Did I do something wrong? I thought you

liked what I was doing."

"No, no, I did. I'm just cold, really." I shivered a little, for effect, as I finally located my sweater and tried to pull it back on. But Jonah stopped me.

"Well, I will warm you up then," Jonah said as he pulled the blanket around me, then squeezed my body closer to his and started kissing my neck again, his hands finding my breasts again. "God, you're so hot."

This *wasn't* just kissing. I could feel his erection growing under me.

"Uh, I have to go to the bathroom," I blurted out before wiggling out of Jonah's embrace. I picked up my bra and sweater and hurried to the bathroom.

When I made it to the bathroom, I turned on the light, put my sweater and bra back on, and stared at myself in the mirror as I gripped the edge of the sink. I looked scared to death. I needed to relax. Taking a couple of deep breaths, I told myself to channel my inner Penny. What would she do in this situation?

Well, she probably wouldn't have minded being stark naked by now.

Maybe I couldn't do that, but I didn't have to be so uptight. This wasn't a big deal. Everyone had sex, especially with their boyfriends. It was just natural. And he *had* called me his girlfriend.

My stomach fluttered at the thought.

After I wiped the terrified expression from my face, I emerged from the bathroom. Jonah had rewound the movie and was sitting on the couch with the TV paused, scrolling through his phone. He was frowning, his brow creased.

I got the feeling he was disappointed in me. I need to do better next time. Or... now. I needed to be sexier, just like the college girls that Jonah probably got with before. *What would Penny do?*

"Listen, I'm sorry for running away earlier. I don't want things to be awkward between us," I blurted out, sitting next to him.

He looked up from his phone. "I just felt like you weren't really enjoying it."

"I was!" When he gave me a doubtful look, I bit my lip. Confession time. "I just really like you, and I'm nervous because I know you've been with other girls, and you're my first...well everything."

His eyes bulged. "I'm your first? You must be lying. A beautiful girl like you has never..."

"No, never. I've never even been kissed. Really, you're like the first guy who's been interested in me." My cheeks flushed.

I held my breath until a crooked smile broke out on his face, and he grabbed my hand. "Well, I'm honored. You're so gorgeous and sexy, and I just wanted to show you tonight how much I like you, Ava."

Jonah had this look in his eye like I was the only thing in the world that he wanted to look at. I couldn't believe he thought I was gorgeous, even after seeing me naked. Well, half-naked anyway. I felt a little better at his reaction. See, this was all a misunderstanding. Now that he knew, he would take things slower.

"I really like you too, Jonah," I said, feeling so much better and braver now. "Did you mean what you said about being my boyfriend?"

He nodded. "Yeah. Ava, I'm really into you. You're so pretty and smart, and you brighten my day whenever I wake up to a text from you."

"Really?" I felt like I was in a dream. How lucky was I?

He nodded again. "Don't look so surprised, Ava. You're really something special." He held up a finger. "Which is what I came over for. D-Phi is having a Halloween blowout this weekend. I thought you'd want to go with me?"

"Seriously?" My jaw dropped, and before he could say more, I blurted, "Yes!" and hugged him. "I'd love to!"

I couldn't fight the goofy grin that came over my face as we watched the rest of the movie side-by-side, with Jonah simply holding my hand. When it was time to leave, he kissed me at the door. "Good night, Ava."

"Good night, Jonah. I had a great time tonight. I'm so glad you surprised me."

And I was. I had a boyfriend now. When I went upstairs to get ready for bed and checked my Instagram, there were selfies of Sara and Penny in the stands, giant slushies in hand, looking like they were having a blast cheering on the Wood Wil Vikings.

I felt a little twang of regret but told myself I'd catch up with them later. I'd bring them to the Halloween party with me, and I knew they'd be thrilled. After all, I had what they wanted—a college boyfriend. And that was so much better.

Chapter Twelve

Halloween was set to be amazing that year, and not just because it happened on a Friday night.

It was because we were all going to a totally epic college party.

I couldn't wait, and neither could the girls. Usually, we went to Penny's house and trick-or-treated around her place since her rich neighbors always used to give the best candy. But that seemed so childish now as we meandered the aisles of Spirit Halloween, adding the finishing touches to our costumes.

"What about this?" Penny said as she held up a tight bustier that looked like it was part of a sexy pirate costume. "Jonah would be your love slave if you showed up in it!"

I fingered the sheer fabric. "Yeah, right! My parents wouldn't let me leave the house if I put that thing on!"

"Besides, we're going as '90's schoolgirls, remember?" I said. That was all we'd talked about. Jonah had decided to dress as a cowboy like he had last year, but I didn't want to be caught wearing a cowboy hat. Plus, I wanted something a little sexier since this was the first time I was being introduced to Jonah's friends as his girlfriend, and I didn't want to look immature. We already had the matching plaid short skirts with suspenders, neon crop tops, neon nail polish, and scrunchies. All we needed were leg warmers.

"Right," Sara said with a smile. "Besides, Ava doesn't need any help. She already has Jonah eating out of the palm of her hand."

I smiled as we picked through a display of neon accessories. I wasn't sure how true that was, but in the past week, my rep at school had definitely improved. Maybe it was just my imagination, but things had shifted in a subtle way. Maybe it was the shot of confidence that Jonah had given me, but now, guys were looking at me. Sara was talking more to *me*, instead of Penny. Even girls I barely spoke to before were asking me to sit next to them. Suddenly, because of Jonah, I was someone.

My whole body was buzzing with excitement and nerves. I suppressed a shiver. "Oh, I'm so nervous!"

Sara said, "Why?"

"No big deal. Now that we're official, he just said he wants me to meet some of his friends. I want to make a good impression."

Penny's jaw dropped. "Oh my God, Ava, that's so big! You're his girlfriend, and he wants to show you off! Why don't you sound more excited?"

"I am excited. I'm just nervous, too." It wasn't a lie.

"Well, don't be nervous. Jonah really likes you. Otherwise, he wouldn't be asking for you to meet his friends. Plus, he's seen you naked. Remember?"

I'd told them the details of our movie date, making it seem slightly spicier than what had really happened. I'd also been a little enigmatic, too, like Penny, leaving some things up to their imagination. Before, my inexperience was pretty obvious since I barely even spoke to any boys. But now that I had Jonah, all bets were off, and I liked to be the one keeping people guessing.

Penny, I think, had gotten the impression that I'd slept with him, and I hadn't bothered to correct her. So, I simply giggled.

Penny had gravitated to neon green and Sara to hot pink, but I liked the neon blue. As I reached for a pair of dangly earrings, my phone began to ring. The girls looked at me expectantly as I fished it out of my pocket. "Jonah?" Sara asked.

I nodded. "Yep. Of course." We were in the habit now of texting on my lunch break and speaking on the phone right after school.

They both gave me an excited look and made themselves scarce so I could take the call. As usual, I got the flutters when I heard his voice. "Hey beautiful. What are you up to?"

"I'm at the store!"

"Oh, is that so?" There was a strange edge to his voice like he was disappointed.

"Yeah. Is something wrong?"

"It's just that you didn't let me know you got home from school, so I wondered."

I laughed. "Okay, Dad."

He sucked in a breath.

"Ava." His voice was hard. He didn't sound angry. He sounded more tired like he was annoyed that I'd changed up the little routine we'd established. "You usually text me at 3:45 to say you're home from school. It's almost 4:30 now, and I've been worried this whole time that something happened to you. Apparently, you're out shopping and didn't even shoot me a text to let me know you were safe?"

I hadn't thought it would be such a big deal, but now, I felt bad for letting him down. "I'm sorry. I was going to text when I got home."

Silence. "I just don't think it's very considerate, Ava."

Now I felt terrible. I'd been so worried about him when he hadn't shown up at the prearranged time to meet my parents. He must've felt the same way. It meant he really cared about me. He was always thinking of me, even when we weren't together.

"I'm sorry, Jonah, I hadn't thought about it that way. We just came to get a few extras for our costumes. I'll be leaving the store soon and I'll be sure to text you as soon as I walk in the house, okay?"

"Yeah, okay."

He sounded so glum. Now, the girls were looking at me from down the aisle. "I can't wait for you to see us in our costumes!" I said brightly. "We are going to look so cute."

A pause. "I thought you were coming alone."

I froze. As if I would do that? It was going to be a huge party. "No... I'm pretty sure I told you Penny and Sara were coming."

"No, you didn't." His voice was flat. "And they weren't really invited."

They were watching me now, confused, so I turned away from them. I didn't see what such a big deal was. They were females, and females were always welcomed at frat parties. "Okay, sorry. But can they?"

He let out a heavy breath. "Listen, Ava. It's not going to be some big party. It's pretty intimate. That's why I invited you. So, you could get to know some of my friends."

"Oh." I swallowed. That was nice and sweet. And I had to go and ruin it, for him and for my friends, by assuming. "I didn't realize. I thought you said it was a blowout. Okay."

"I'm sure you're going to look so hot. You're so beautiful. You will stand out in any costume. I just hope that we are on the same page with each other. I don't want to introduce you to my friends if we don't feel the same way about each other."

He sounded very serious and mature, and suddenly, I felt like an idiot for getting my friends' hopes up. *Of course*, they weren't invited. Who gets invited by their boyfriend to a party and insists on having her friends tag along? I was such a naïve idiot.

"We are! I really like you, Jonah. I want to meet your friends, and I really hope they like me." I stopped babbling, wondering if he even liked me now. I was so stupid. Why had I messed everything up like that? "You know that, right?"

"I'm not sure, to be honest. I thought you really liked me, but it didn't feel that way today. When you didn't call, I didn't know what to think. I think about you all the time, and I would never want you to worry. Just makes me think we aren't on the same page with how we feel about each other."

I could hear the hurt in Jonah's voice, and it was like a knife twisting deep inside me. I had to be better. To show him I cared.

"No, no, we are on the same page! I think about you all the time, too. Really," I said, scanning the shelves with zero interest now. Our fun Halloween night felt a lot less so now. But it would be fine. I'd be with Jonah, meeting his friends. And my best friends would understand.

"So, I'll pick you up at around nine, then?" he asked.

"Yeah. Sounds good."

There was a long pause since my head was filled with worries about how Penny and Sara would take this bad news.

"I'll always worry about you, Ava. I really care about you," he said to me, which melted my heart. Everything was okay.

I ended the call and turned to look at them, but from their faces, they already knew. Penny sighed. "So, what? Did he uninvite us?"

"It's not that. I thought it was a big party. But apparently, it's going to be pretty small," I said with a shrug. "Sorry."

Sara looked at the neon socks in her hands. "Well, that blows."

"Hey, maybe you can ask Kyle and Biggs to invite you?" I suggested.

Sara snorted and said, "Biggs, who? I haven't seen Biggs in weeks. You know he basically ghosted me."

I looked at Penny. She'd told me she and Kyle had been texting on and off and that she was looking forward to seeing him again. But she wrinkled her nose.

"God, Ava, who do you think I am? I'm not going to beg Kyle

to invite me to a party. Talk about pathetic." She shrugged. "Besides, I don't think he is even going to be there. He mentioned having to go home this weekend for a family thing. So, of course, he wouldn't invite me."

"What about Ben? Maybe if you asked him, he could—"

Penny snorted. "It was like pulling teeth to get him to let me go the last time."

Sara added, "Right. And I don't want to go there if it's going to be small. Talk about awkward."

"And I bet Ava doesn't even want us to come," Penny said, talking only to Sara as if I wasn't even there. "We're not as cool as she is with her college boyfriend."

Sara nodded, and I let out a groan. "What? Pen, it's not like—"

"It's fine, Ava. Have fun with your boyfriend. But, when you get home, try to remember that you do have friends outside of your relationship."

Okay, that stung, especially since I'd really wanted them to come. But I tried not to show it.

"You know I love you guys. We can hang out again soon!" I suggested, trying to be enthusiastic. "Maybe next weekend?"

"Yeah. Sure." Then Penny linked her arm through Sara's and dragged her away from me. "Let's get matching scarves. It might be cold while we're trick-or-treating."

Chapter Thirteen

Shortly after nine that Friday, I finished putting the scrunchie in my hair and went downstairs to where my parents were relaxing on the couch after a busy evening of handing out candy.

"Bye, guys!" I shouted, reaching for the door.

My mother didn't look up from her phone, which I was glad about, considering my outfit was a little skimpy. "Are you sure this party is going to be safe?"

"It's not a party, just a get-together. My friends will be there. And Jonah is safe," I said, looking out at his car. He had parked in the driveway, his headlights blinding me. It was a lie about Sara and Penny, but my mom had been on the fence about letting me go, so I needed all the help I could get. If she found out they weren't there, I could just say that our wires got crossed. "See you."

"Home by midnight," she said, to my chagrin. According to Jonah, midnight was when the best parties got started. But this wasn't a party. Just a get-together. He would understand.

"Sure. Bye."

When I ran out and opened the door, Jonah tipped his obnoxiously big cowboy hat and said, "Howdy, ma'am. Don't you look mighty fine this evening?"

I couldn't help but burst out laughing. He was all dressed up in cowboy attire, complete with a hat, button-down shirt, jeans, and even cowboy boots.

"Well, thank you. I can't believe you have cowboy boots!"

"There's a lot of things about me that you wouldn't believe," Jonah said as he leaned over the console to give me a kiss. "You look good enough to eat."

The ride in Jonah's car was just like any other. The music played, and Jonah held my hand the whole way. When we pulled up to the frat house, I looked down at our intertwined hands and then up at Jonah's face. It was nice being like this. I was already so comfortable with him, and now he was officially my boyfriend. *I could get used to this.*

Jonah caught me smiling and said, "I have a surprise for you before we go in."

He reached into the backseat to grab a small gift bag topped with tissue paper. Smiling, I removed the tissue paper and found a small, square jewelry box. When I opened the box, I found a thin gold chain with a pendant of two intertwined hearts: one gold and one silver.

"Wow, Jonah. This is so beautiful. You really didn't have to get this for me."

"You see, the two hearts represent our hearts. We are two hearts that are now intertwined and bound together. I want you to wear it every day so that you know I'm always with you right here," Jonah touched the center of my chest right where my heart should be.

My eyes started to tear up because I'd never had anyone say anything so beautiful to me. I would never take this necklace off. Never.

"I love it. I'll wear it everywhere! Can you help me with it?" I asked, taking it out and handing it to him. I turned away from him, lifting my hair, and when he gently slid it on and fastened the clasp, I turned back, modeling it for his approval.

"My God, Ava, you look so beautiful with that necklace on." He leaned over and kissed me. At first, I thought it was going to be a light kiss, which was fine since I didn't want to mess up my make-up before I met his friends.

"I'm so glad you like it because I want all my friends to know how I feel about you, and this necklace will show them that you are mine and mine only," he said when he pulled away, putting his hand on my thigh.

"I love it," I said, ready to go and meet them.

But then he moved in for another kiss, and before I knew it, we were full-on making out. And he kept sliding his hand up my thigh until his fingers were under my skirt, brushing against my underwear. We were parked right outside the frat house, though. Not exactly private. What if someone saw us? But I had no way of pulling away. The force of Jonah's kisses was pushing my back into the seat.

That was when Jonah slowly started to run his fingers over my underwear and between my legs. Tension coiled in my chest as he let out a little groan like he had no intention of stopping anytime soon. And anyone could walk by and see us. I didn't want his friends seeing me like this before I'd even met them.

So, I wiggled my head until I'd broken away from Jonah's mouth. "Um, aren't we supposed to go inside?"

"We'll go when we're ready, and you look too good for me to be ready to go mingle." Jonah leaned toward me again.

"Okay, but it's just...what if someone sees us?"

Jonah chuckled and said, "Alright, alright. Looks like someone needs a drink."

I was glad he didn't seem angry, but I wasn't really sure what he meant. I hoped he didn't think that getting me drunk would change my mind about sex. This was supposed to be a big day for us, meeting his friends and being accepted into his life. I didn't need that extra complication hovering over the night.

Contrary to what Jonah had said, it didn't look like a small get-together. In fact, the party looked similar to the last, with crowds of people waiting to get inside. As we went to climb the steps, I said, "It doesn't look very intimate."

He hitched his shoulder. "Well, you know how these things go. Sometimes word spreads."

Disappointment coiled inside me. So, I could've brought my friends. I only hoped Penny and Sara didn't find out about this. If they did, they'd probably think I'd lied, so they wouldn't come.

Because I was with Jonah this time, I was able to skip the line, which gave me a surge of pride. But other than that, it was the same as the last party. Lots of people I didn't know, the smell of beer in the air, my shoes sticking to the floor as I followed Jonah around the house. When Jonah was waved over by a guy in an Icana Football jersey at the beer pong game, I stood behind Jonah as he spoke, waiting for him to introduce me, but he never did. After he finished his conversation, he walked me over to the keg and poured us each a beer.

"This is a great song. Do you want to dance?" Jonah asked.

"Um, okay. Sure."

Jonah threw back his drink and grabbed me by the waist, nudging me through the crowd to the makeshift dance floor. Holding on to my drink, I tried to keep up with the pulsating crowd without spilling it, but I was jostled all over the place, and most of it ended up on the ground or down the front of my costume.

After a couple of songs, Jonah leaned in. "You're out? One second. I'll be right back."

Before I could tell him I didn't want another one, he headed off toward the keg, leaving me alone.

At first, I tried to just enjoy myself. This was my boyfriend's house, and he was a brother here. But after a while, I looked at all the older college kids hanging out in groups and began to feel like an outsider again. I stared at my empty cup, wondering how many songs had played since Jonah had told me he'd be right back. Then I stood on my toes and looked around the room, thinking he must've forgotten where he left me. He wasn't by the keg. The house was pretty big, so I wasn't sure where he'd gone.

I wandered toward the kitchen. I saw the guy Jonah had been talking to before, still playing beer pong, and thought about asking him, but he seemed too absorbed in the game and too drunk. I noticed that the back door was open, and people were going in and out, so I went out there.

There was a firepit outside with a raging fire, and people huddled around it. I stood at the top stairs, squinting in the dark, trying to make out Jonah's cowboy hat.

Just when I was sure he wasn't there, I noticed someone familiar sitting on an old lounge chair. It was Kyle. He had a beer in one hand and was being straddled by a girl who was dressed like a sexy cat.

I gaped, unable to look away. What happened to him going away for a family thing? Good thing Penny wasn't here. She'd be devastated. It looked like Kyle and this girl were hardcore making out, and from the way she was grinding against him in the darkness, it almost looked as if they were having sex right out in the open.

At least Jonah and I had been in a car. Maybe I was being stupid, worrying about anyone seeing us. Maybe that was just what people did, and now Jonah was angry at me for being so immature.

I also had to wonder if that was why Jonah didn't want Penny to be there. Maybe his brothers had told him that Penny wasn't welcome. I had no way of knowing.

"Hey. Where'd you go off to?" A voice said behind me.

I let out a gasp of relief when I saw Jonah. He was holding two beers. He handed one to me, but I didn't take a sip.

He frowned. "You don't look like you're getting any looser."

No. I wasn't. In fact, I kind of wanted to go home. He'd told me this was a low-key thing, an intimate party where I'd get to know the people close to him, but that wasn't true. But I touched the necklace at my throat and tried to think rationally. "Well, I couldn't find you. And I thought you were going to introduce me to your friends?"

He held up a finger and looked around, and when he did, I realized that his eyes were bleary. How many beers did he have while we were apart?

Then he grabbed my arm and led me toward the fire. We sat down next to each other on a bench there, with a few guys hanging around the fire, laughing and tossing back a bottle of vodka. A tall, dark-haired guy came over to us and plopped down on the bench next to Jonah.

"Hey man, looks like you found her," Mark said, leaning forward to look at me.

"Mark, this is my gorgeous girlfriend, Ava. Ava, this is my friend Mark," Jonah said.

"Best friend, actually! I've known this idiot this we were in preschool. Ain't that right, Jo Jo?"

"We've known each other maybe a bit too long." The boys cracked up, leaving me out of the joke.

We chatted a little more. Actually, *they* chatted like the good friends they were, about people and things I didn't understand, and I mostly listened and nursed my beer. I'd been reading what I would say when people asked me where I went to school—*I'm headed off to college next year*—so that I wouldn't sound too immature. But Mark never asked. He never asked me anything. Either he already knew, or he didn't care. After a while, I finished the entire cup. I think the only time Mark noticed me was when I was setting the cup down on the ground.

He stood up. "Your lady here looks thirsty. Let me run and grab her a drink really quick. Is beer okay?"

I nodded.

No sooner had Mark jogged back into the house than Jonah put his arm around my waist and pulled me closer so I was flush against him. I liked the warmth radiating from his body, especially since it was getting colder and I was still only in a crop top.

Just as I was warming up next to Jonah, he turned his head toward my neck. I had been worried about being seen before, but after seeing that girl with Kyle, and because the beer was working its magic, I didn't mind so much. In fact, I liked it. His lips were incredibly soft and warm on my cool neck as he kissed along my collarbone. He gently scooped the chain of my necklace up with his tongue and fidgeted with it a moment before moving his mouth up to my ear.

"My God, you are so stunning, Ava. I've never met anyone as beautiful as you."

I felt warmth bubble up inside me as I turned my head, and my lips found his. The kiss was slow at first, but I could tell Jonah wanted more. Even here, surrounded by all these people, it felt like we were alone. Or I didn't care. I pressed myself against him and wrapped my hands around his neck, caressing his head and running my fingers through his hair.

Then I felt the pressure of Jonah's hands on the outsides of my thighs. Before I knew it, he'd lifted me up onto his lap. The movement was so swift that it didn't break our kiss in the slightest. It felt like we had been kissing for a few moments when Jonah finally broke away and leaned his forehead against mine, his breath wavering slightly from the intensity of our kiss.

"Well, well, well. Someone's having a little too much fun out here," a voice said behind me.

I slid off Jonah's lap and back to my spot next to him as Mark handed me the beer. I chugged it almost immediately as the guys chatted more about old stories I knew nothing about.

I sat there, trying to listen, but my head started to get foggier and foggier. I couldn't quite focus on Mark's face as he spoke. I couldn't pick up on anything they were talking about, so instead, I grabbed Jonah's hand to let him know I was there and I was trying.

After what felt like hours, Jonah stood up, his hand still wrapped around mine, so I rose too as Jonah said his goodbye to Mark.

"It was nice to meet you, Ava," Mark said, giving me a nod.

"You too."

Well, I'd met one of his friends. That was something. But he hadn't been particularly nice or friendly to me. He'd seemed more interested in chumming it up with Jonah. I felt a little like a third wheel.

Maybe that was my problem, for being shy. Maybe I should've inserted myself in the conversation more.

I'd do that next time. Somehow. I felt a little braver now, with alcohol in my veins.

But as we climbed the steps, my phone buzzed with a text. I pulled it out, thinking it was Penny, asking how everything was going. I couldn't wait to send her a photo of the necklace Jonah had given me.

Instead, I saw a text from my Mom. *Where are you?*

The sight instantly scared me sober. I looked at the time. It was ten after twelve.

Oh, my God. I'd blown curfew.

The party, however, didn't look anywhere near over. In fact, it was more crowded than ever and seemed to be just getting started.

I stopped as we reached the door. "Jonah, I have to—"

He wasn't listening, though. My voice was swallowed up by the thumping bass. I tugged on his arm as he reached for a couple more beers, and he finally looked back at me.

"Jonah. I'm sorry. I have to go." I pointed to my phone.

He nodded. "No worries."

Then he led me back through the house, stopping occasionally to say goodbye to a few other people. He didn't introduce me to anyone other than Mark, and that was fine because now I wanted to leave as soon as possible. But he seemed to be taking the scenic route, strolling leisurely with my hand in his. *Showing me off,* like Penny had said. I should've felt good about that.

And yet, somehow, I felt invisible. I just stood behind him, hand in his hand, waiting until he pulled me along to the next room. I was afraid that if I told him to hurry, he'd remember just how immature I was with my stupid curfew.

I was silently cursing my parents for being so strict when we finally made it out the door. Jonah walked me slowly across the lawn to where his car was parked, taking all the time in the world, and held the door open for me.

"What?" he said because my face probably told how nervous I was.

I glanced at my phone. 1:02. I was a full hour late. "Nothing. I mean, it's fine," I said as I typed in a message to my mom. *Sorry. Lost track of time. We're heading home now.*

"I don't think you ever loosened up," he remarked as he pulled away from the curb. "Too bad. Didn't you have fun?"

I might have, if you made an effort to introduce me to more of your friends and make me feel like I belonged there, I thought.

But I didn't say it. Instead, I said, "Um, well..."

"Next time, you'll just have to pry that stick out of your ass," he said. "Maybe then you'll have fun."

Shocked by those words, I blushed. I touched the pendant on my throat and tried to think of all the good that had happened since I knew that when I saw my parents again, it would be *bad*. They might not even let me see Jonah again. And then what would I do?

He was looking at me expectantly, so I just smiled. "No. I did have fun. It was amazing."

Chapter Fourteen

I thought my parents would ground me after coming home late, but they were surprisingly okay with it. *These things happen,* my father had said when I came in the door. *Just don't let it happen again.* I guess Jonah was right. He'd easily won them over.

The biggest problem I faced that weekend was what I would tell Penny about seeing Kyle. I kept expecting that she would text me to see how the party went, but she never did, so by Sunday night, I wondered if she was angrier at me than she was letting on.

I had just finished brushing my teeth and was walking back to my bedroom, thinking about that, when I got a text from Jonah. *Wear something sexy to school today. I want everyone to be jealous when I pick you up* 😊 *I'll be there at 3:30 sharp!*

I smiled. This time, everyone would see me walk out of the front door of that cement prison and into Jonah's arms. They'd all whisper about how lucky I was. I could live with that.

Despite everything with Sara and Penny, I was in a good mood as I went into the lunchroom that afternoon. I'd spent too long rummaging through my closet to find the perfect sexy outfit that wouldn't get me sent to the principal's office—tight jeans and a sheer tank top with a black bra underneath, and judging by the looks I was getting from other guys, I looked good. I couldn't wait for Jonah to see me.

But when I reached the lunch table, Penny and Sara were already there, so wrapped up in their conversation that they didn't even look at me.

"... and I was like, how many times can you say Marco Polo before I smack it out of your mouth!" Penny said, to which Sara laughed.

"What are you talking about?" I asked, sitting across from them.

Penny glanced over at me. "Oh. Nothing. You wouldn't get it." She inspected my outfit but didn't tell me how hot it was, which was unlike her. "How was your Halloween, girl?"

"Good," I said, certain they'd ask me more. But they didn't. After a long pause, I asked, "Did you two have fun trick-or-treating?"

Sara and Penny exchanged glances, and then both burst out laughing.

"That's not all we did," Sara said, and the two grinned conspiratorially at one another as if they were sharing a big secret.

I couldn't help but be interested. Not to mention, I felt a little left out. "What?"

"One of Penny's neighbors had an indoor pool. He was so *hot*. He and his friends invited us to go skinny dipping," Sara whispered. "It was so much fun!"

My jaw dropped. So much for worrying about Penny being devastated about Kyle. She'd moved on, too. "Oh, wow... so who are these guys? Are you going to see them again?"

"Maybe," Penny said and then looked at Sara. "Outlook's positive."

They burst out laughing again. I felt like I had missed a huge part of this conversation, so I just said, "That's cool."

"So, how were Jonah's friends?" Penny asked me, digging into her salad.

I couldn't say. Mark was okay, if a little self-absorbed. Other than that, I hadn't been introduced to anyone else. "Great. Really nice. I had a really good time," I lied.

"So, it goes without saying you're going to see him again?" Penny asked.

"He's picking me up after school." I glanced at the clock. Only two more hours.

"Oh. *That's* why you look like that," Penny said with a sly grin. I couldn't tell if that was a compliment or an insult.

"But I thought we could do something this weekend?" I blurted, just so they wouldn't think I'd totally checked out of our friendship. "Maybe a girl's spa day?"

They didn't answer right away. Instead, they both looked at each other as if they weren't sure they wanted to hang out with me again. Then Penny smiled. "Sure. That will be fun."

I felt a little bit better after that. I'd seen so many girls lose themselves to the boys they were dating and had told myself that would never be me. I would not let my relationship with Jonah intrude on my time with my friends.

I was jittery when the final bell rang, and I grabbed my backpack to head outside. When I made it to the side doors, there he was.

He was parked right in front of the pick-up parking lot, leaning on the hood of his car with his arms crossed. He looked so confident just standing there, waiting for me. My stomach jumped. I picked up the pace and practically skipped over to him.

As I got closer, Jonah's head swiveled toward me, and our eyes locked. A smile broke across his face. He looked me up and down as I walked closer to him, reaching one arm around my waist and the other up to cup my cheek. Everything around us disappeared. He gave me a lingering kiss that I felt in my toes before pulling away and saying, "My God, Ava, you look stunning."

I blushed and he gave me a little toss of the head, like he couldn't believe how lucky he was to be looking at me. That smile made me feel like the only girl in the world.

The wind blew, making me shudder since I hadn't brought a

coat because I hadn't wanted to ruin the effect of the outfit.

"Ah, are you cold, little lady?" Jonah asked as he wrapped his arms tighter around me.

"Just a little."

"Well, let me warm you up."

Jonah rubbed his hands up and down my back. I could feel the warmth of his hands through my sheer shirt.

After a moment, Jonah whispered, "Still cold?"

I didn't want him to stop. "A bit," I said as I dropped my head onto Jonah's shoulder. He kept rubbing his hands on my back, a little slower this time.

After a minute, he said, "Are you ready to go? I was thinking we could stop for ice cream."

"I'd love to."

He opened the door for me, and I climbed into his old Audi, and we made our way to the local ice cream shop, The Scoop. Since it was the first week of November, the sky was starting to darken as we pulled into the near-empty parking lot. Inside, Jonah paid for our ice cream and suggested we eat in the car.

"So, what did your friends think about me?" I asked as we sat side-by-side in the car, digging into my hot fudge sundae.

"What do you mean?" Jonah seemed confused.

"From the party. I was wondering what people said about me."

"Oh, right." He shrugged. "Well, those people weren't really good friends or anything. I honestly don't know them very well."

That was odd. I could've sworn he knew those people pretty well since they were all talking to him. "Oh, okay. I mean, you were talking to quite a few people, and you mentioned you wanted me to come to meet everyone."

"Did you not have a good time, Ava?" Jonah licked the last bit of ice cream off his spoon.

I sensed he was getting a little upset, so I spoke as gently as possible. "No, I had a lot of fun. I just thought you wanted me to meet some of your friends, but when we were at the party, I felt like I didn't really talk to anyone."

"Yeah, like I said, I didn't know most of those people very well. They're fun to hang out with, but that's about it."

"Okay, I see." I fiddled with my necklace, still feeling unsettled.

"They might be my brothers, but we're not close. Mark is really the only one that I cared about you meeting at that party. We've been friends since we were babies, and his opinion means a lot to me."

"Oh, okay," I said, perking up. "So, what did he say about me then?"

"Nothing, really. He just said he was jealous I was dating such a hottie." He smirked at me and leaned in for a kiss.

I hadn't finished my ice cream, so I propped the dish between my legs and kissed him back. The kiss started out slowly, and I could taste the chocolate syrup on his tongue and feel the warm air from the vent blowing on my face. Soon enough, Jonah's hand was cupping my face, and his lips were pressing more firmly onto mine. I felt a little rush of excitement, loving the way our lips complemented each other and the way he'd softly lick my lips between kisses. *It's like we're made for each other.*

I broke away from Jonah's lips and smiled. "You're such a good kisser, Jonah."

"It takes practice." He smirked.

"I've never kissed anyone but you." I blushed as I looked down at my ice cream. It had melted into soup.

"Well, I'm happy to practice with you any time."

I wanted to keep practicing with him, but as he leaned in to kiss me again, I couldn't help wondering how many other girls he had kissed.

I put a hand on his chest. "Have you kissed many other girls?"

He stopped and considered this as if he had never been asked the question before. "Yeah. But none of them compares to you, Ava."

Something clawed at my chest, a rush of insecurity. I don't know why. I knew Jonah could get with just about any girl he wanted. But hearing it was a different story.

My disappointment must have shown on my face because he added, "You know, nothing meaningful or lasting. That's why you're different."

"But you said you had a girlfriend before me."

Jonah sighed and glanced out the window. "I dated one other girl seriously back in high school."

That clawing feeling got worse. *Back in high school.* He made it seem like a thousand years ago, like I was so young in comparison to him. "She was your first kiss then?"

"She was my first everything."

That clawing feeling seemed to grip my throat. I swallowed. "What do you mean, 'everything'?"

"You know, she was the first girl I asked on a date, who I kissed, who I slept with and all that."

I felt like I'd been punched in the stomach. I'd only just had my first kiss a few weeks ago, and he'd slept with a girl. I'd guessed he probably had. He was 21, after all, but still...

My heart started to pound. "So, is that the only person you slept with then?"

"Yeah, she's the only one so far. I just haven't found the right person to have that experience with again. I want to feel a connection with someone before I take on a big step like that."

I let out the breath I'd been holding. Okay. At least he was looking for more than just a good time with someone. Still, what if I didn't meet Jonah's expectations? What if I was terrible at it? What if he slept with me and couldn't stop thinking of how I compared to his old girlfriend?

"Are you finished with your ice cream?"

I nodded, happy he broke the silence as he picked up the cup and got out of the car to throw it away. I didn't know what to say.

Jonah got back in the car. "Let's get you home, huh? I'm sure you have a ton of homework."

The ride home was not awkward at all. He told me about the internship he was about to start during the short drive back to my house, so I really didn't have to speak at all. I was still collecting my thoughts when Jonah pulled into the driveway.

"So, should I come over this weekend?"

"Uh," I stammered. "Actually. Maybe? The girls wanted to do something this weekend. I'm not sure when."

"Who? Penny and Sara?"

"Yeah, they wanted to have a girl's night and do face masks or whatever. I thought it'd be relaxing."

"That sounds nice. You should do that with your friends." Jonah smiled, but I could tell he was a little disappointed. "Just let me know when you're free this weekend then."

I promised I would and gave him a quick kiss before heading out the door. It was a delicate balance, keeping both my boyfriend and my friends happy. For now, I thought I had done it, so I was relieved.

But I guess I wasn't as smart as I'd thought.

Chapter Fifteen

A week before Thanksgiving, as I waited in homeroom for school to begin, I stared at the message from Barb, my supervisor at the Seagreen Valley Animal Shelter.

Haven't seen your smiling face in months! Just wondering if I should keep you on our volunteer roster.

I squirmed under the weight of my guilt. I'd totally let my volunteering go this year, only making one Saturday morning weeks ago. I imagined all the poor pups and kitties I'd been neglecting, and my heart sank, especially knowing I wouldn't be able to volunteer in the coming weekend since I had planned to do things with Jonah.

I typed in: *Keep me on the schedule! I'm going to try to come in sometime in December. Thanks!*

Then I went to the last message I'd received from Jonah, hoping it would make me feel better.

And it did. *Good night, gorgeous.* He'd sent it to me last night, but it still made my stomach flutter at the thought of him sending it.

We had been getting closer and closer. Usually, he'd pick me up after school, and we'd go to the ice cream shop or to the Rockhill Mall just to walk around. Time seemed to go by so fast when we were together. I never wanted it to end.

Even though it was only five hours until I'd see him again, the school day ahead seemed to drag on endlessly. I'd gone through most of my sexiest outfits and hadn't had time to wash anything, so I wasn't sure about the skirt I was wearing. I bought it at the Rockhill Mall because Jonah had said how hot I'd look in it. I thought it was okay when I put it on, but judging from the looks I'd gotten in the hallway, it might have been a tad too short for school.

When the bell for homeroom rang, and Mr. Harper walked in, eyes firmly on me, I knew I was in trouble.

He went to his desk and pulled out a bag of clothes from the lost and found, grabbing a pair of ugly, bulky gray sweatpants. "Ava. You're our lucky winner."

I groaned as people snickered around me and pulled at the hem of the denim skirt. "It's not that short."

He rapped on his desk. "Don't give me that. Come on. Up. Get changed in the ladies' room."

When I stood up, I felt a rush of air go up my skirt, so yes, it probably *was* that short. But Jonah had been telling me I had the nicest legs, and I'd gotten a lot of confidence as a result. It still didn't stop me from blushing when I turned around to grab my bag and saw a bunch of guys staring at me and smirking.

Stupid high school boys. That's what Penny had always called them, and she was right. Their opinion didn't mean anything to me now. I glared at them.

I grabbed the sweatpants from Mr. Harper and trudged across the hallway to the girls' bathroom. I went into a stall and pulled the sweatpants on over my hips, then slid the skirt down. The sweatpants were three sizes too big and smelled like stale air, but whatever. I'd change back into the skirt before I saw Jonah. No problem.

I was about to unlatch the stall lock and step out when I heard the outside door fly open. Someone rushed past my stall and threw the door next to mine closed so hard that all of them rattled. I heard a bag fall to the ground, then saw the shadow of someone falling to her knees in front of the toilet. The poor girl retched, again and again, before there was the obvious sound of whatever she'd had for breakfast splashing into the bowl.

I winced, wanting to help but not wanting to intrude on her. I'd be mortified if anyone came in on me, getting sick in the school bathroom. So, I just stood there for a minute, wondering what to do, as the girl continued to vomit.

Then she kind of let out a pitiful moan and collapsed onto the tile floor, so all I could see under the door was her backside and lower back.

Something about her sweater was familiar. It was baby blue, just like a one that Penny had. In fact...

My breath hitched. "Penny?" I ventured.

There was silence, but the girl in the next stall straightened, and I could hear her climbing to her feet. Then the toilet flushed. "Ava?"

"Yeah." I pulled on the latch and stepped out, just as she did, wiping her mouth with a bit of toilet paper. "You okay?"

"Sure. Just skipped breakfast." She was already looking in the mirror and fumbling through her bag for her lip oil. "Ugh. Staying thin is not for the faint of heart."

I gave her a look. She didn't meet my eyes, not even in the mirror. She was avoiding me. "Are you telling me you've decided to become bulimic?"

"I'm gaining weight like crazy," she said, putting away her lip oil and fluffing her hair. "I have to do *something*."

I studied her. Something was off. She looked different. Her eyes were red like she'd been crying. And Penny, not eat? She pretended to be the dainty eater at school with her tiny side salads, but the girl loved food. She was known to eat a whole roll of cookie dough in one sitting. She didn't skip meals. *Ever*.

And she still wasn't looking at me. She reached around me to toss away the wadded ball of toilet paper. "What?" she mumbled, since I was staring hard at her.

"Something's up with you," I said. "I'm trying to figure out what it is."

She snorted. "Maybe you would know if you spent more time with me instead of with Jonah."

Was that jealousy? Okay, the last time I'd been with her and Sara was for the spa date almost two weeks earlier. We'd had fun, but it didn't feel like old times. It almost felt like we were forcing ourselves to have a good time. As if our worlds had gotten larger, and now we all had other places we'd rather be. "Don't try to send me on this guilt trip. I asked you last weekend if you wanted to hang out."

She rolled her eyes. "On a Sunday. I had homework."

"But I tried. I don't know what you want from—"

She grabbed her backpack from the stall and moved past me. "Don't worry about it. Don't—" Her face went ashen. She threw her bag down at my feet and rushed into the stall, retching again. This time, when she finished, she let out a sob. When I came over to check on her, her voice echoed into the bowl, since she was draped over it, her hair hanging in. "Just go away, Ava."

I probably could have. I didn't feel like I'd done anything wrong. But it hurt me that Penny was so down about our drifting apart. I didn't want it to happen. And it didn't have to. I could save this.

Steeling myself, I pulled open the door and went into the stall. "No. I'm not going away," I said, leaning over and gathering her hair so she wouldn't puke on it. "If you're sick, let me help you."

"I'm not sick," she said softly.

I almost laughed. How could she say that with her head stuck in a toilet? She wasn't forcing herself to throw up. She was most definitely sick. She was—

I froze as it suddenly occurred to me. "Are you...? Do you

mean you're...?" I couldn't say the word.

"Late." The word floated up.

All I could do was stare at the back of my best friend's head in shock. As much as Penny tried to act older than all of us, she was still just a kid like me. She might have been close to 18, but I couldn't see her as a mother to a baby.

"Oh." It came out as a breath. "What are you going to do?"

Stupid question. I was sure she didn't know.

She fumbled for the toilet paper. "I need to go to Vernon this afternoon. The Rite-Aid is there. I'll get one of those tests that you pee on."

I ripped a few squares and handed it to her. Apparently, she'd already thought it through. Vernon was the next town over, far away enough that no one we knew would be there. It made sense, but she'd need moral support for it.

I had been looking forward to seeing Jonah, but I couldn't abandon Penny. I reached into my bag, looking for a granola bar or something to give her so she wouldn't be sick again. But I didn't have anything. Just gum. I offered her a stick. "I'll come with you."

She looked up at me gratefully and took the gum, unwrapping it and feeding it into her mouth. "Thanks," she said as she chewed.

I helped get her up and stayed with her while she fixed her make-up, and then we made plans for her to drive us to Vernon that afternoon. When we separated, as the bell for first period rang, I hurried to type in a text to Jonah. *Hey. I have to go somewhere this afternoon with Penny. I'll call you when I'm done, and maybe we can meet up then?*

He wouldn't be happy at first, but he'd understand once I explained things to him.

. The message registered as "read" almost the moment I sent it to him. But he never responded at all.

Chapter Sixteen

I stood near the sinks in the bathroom of the Vernon Dunkin', simultaneously sipping a vanilla iced latte and obsessively checking my phone for a message from Jonah as I waited for Penny to come out with the verdict. Tapping my boot on the tile floor, I glared at the display. *Read,* it said. Then why didn't he respond?

He was probably pissed at me. I itched to explain things, but I couldn't do it over text.

And Penny was taking too long. I'd heard her pee ten minutes ago. "Everything okay in there?"

"Uh-huh," she mumbled, flushing the toilet.

Jonah was taking too long, too. Why wasn't he texting back? Getting impatient, I texted, *Almost done here. Do you want to meet up later?*

Once again, it immediately registered as "read." But no response. I let out a little groan of frustration. What was with these games? I'd canceled with him because I had an actual emergency. My friend was in need.

But he didn't know that. Once he heard my excuse, I was sure all would be forgiven. *If* I ever got out of here.

The door opened, and Penny stepped out, looking smaller and more fragile than I'd ever seen her. She was holding the pregnancy test wand out in front of her as if it was infected, her phone in her other hand. "It says we have to wait fifteen minutes. It's only been ten."

I inspected the little display window. There were already two lines, one slightly fainter than the other. Next to it, there was a key that showed two lines meant pregnant. "Um. Can there be a false positive?"

She squinted at it. "I don't think so." She swallowed. "Shit. How could this happen? We were always safe."

"You mean..." I paused, trying to think of the most diplomatic way to ask. "It's definitely Kyle's?"

She glared at me. "Of course it is. I haven't been with anyone else."

As she washed her hands, I glanced at my phone again. Still no message from Jonah. "Are you going to tell him?"

She nodded and grabbed some paper towels from the dispenser. "Obviously. He needs to know he's going to be a father."

"You're not just going to...?" I couldn't say the word *abortion.* "You want to go to a clinic and be sure first?"

She took one last look at the pregnancy test before wrapping it in the wad of paper towel and tossing it away as if that would help her get rid of the problem. "I guess I should. Where's the nearest one?"

I had spent the half-hour drive to Rite-Aid looking on my phone. "It's here, actually, in Vernon. I can go with you. Do you want to call and make an—"

"I think I should get home. I have homework to do," she said, grabbing her bag. "I'll figure it out. I'm so tired. I think I need to sleep on it."

She was putting on that tough exterior, but I could tell she was close to crumbling. There was something so fragile about her, like a single touch would send her to pieces. "Hey. It's going to be okay."

"I know," she said tightly. Then she smiled. "Actually, this is a good thing. Kyle won't be able to ignore my texts anymore when I tell him I'm having his baby. Right?"

Despite her certainty, I wasn't so sure about that. "I guess."

"Cool. Are you seeing Jonah later or what?" she asked me as we went outside to her car.

I was about to say I wasn't sure, but just at that moment, my phone buzzed with a text. It was Jonah. *Pick you up at your house at six?*

Despite the tense situation with Penny, I smiled. *Sounds great!*

Then I looked up, smiling goofily, and realized Penny hadn't pulled out of the parking space yet. She was just looking at me, expectant.

She'd asked me a question. What was it? Oh. "Yeah. That was him. We're meeting up tonight."

She tossed her hair and looked in the rear-view mirror. "Fun," she muttered in the least excited voice possible.

I gave her a pass on that. Her whole life was changing because of a guy. Even though she'd asked, she didn't really want to hear about my relationship with Jonah, especially since things between us were going so well. Jonah wasn't with me, just for sex. Sure, he'd pressured me a lot, but whenever I told him I wasn't ready, he always respected that.

As we drove, I was silent, thinking about what Jonah would do had we ended up in the same situation. He always told me how much he never wanted to hurt me and how thankful he was to have me in his life. Of course, he'd want me to keep the baby. He was a senior, due to graduate in a few months. He never talked much about his business, and I really didn't understand what it was that he did, but he did say it was starting to take off. And when we went out, he always had plenty of money to treat me.

I imagined we'd get married, maybe get an apartment downtown.

A nervous excitement fluttered through me when I thought about having a place with Jonah. He'd come home to me and the baby, briefcase in hand, and give us each a kiss. Then, he'd take over baby duty while I went to college.

It wouldn't be easy, but thinking of our little family still made my insides fizz with happiness.

When Penny pulled up at my house, Jonah's silver car was already parked in the driveway. It was a few minutes before six. He was early.

Penny said, "Well, look who it is," with a slight note of annoyance in her voice.

"Oh. I told him to meet me here," I said, already pulling my seatbelt off and reaching for the door handle. "I'll call you tonight to see how you are."

She nodded. "Thanks for everything, babe," she said, and for a second, I thought I saw that old, confident Penny.

She sped off, and I rushed over to Jonah's car. I could see him sitting in the driver's seat, so I pulled open the door and slid in.

"Hey!" I leaned over to give him a kiss, but he didn't lean in to meet me. He looked stiff. I wound up awkwardly brushing the side of his cheek with my lips. "Everything okay?"

He threw the car in reverse to pull out of the driveway. "Why wouldn't it be?"

Even that sounded wrong. "I don't know. Are you angry that I had to go with Penny?"

"Who said I was angry?"

He sounded angry. "Well, she really needed me. She was having a bit of a crisis. I had to help out."

He didn't say anything. He didn't stop at a stop sign and took a turn with frightening speed, making me grasp the door handle.

I hadn't planned to tell him about Penny yet. I thought I should at least wait until Kyle knew first. But he was making me nervous. I had to make him understand. Besides, I trusted him. The secret would be safe with him.

"Yeah," I continued conversationally. "Don't tell anyone I told you, but would you believe Penny just found out she's pregnant. She's so upset."

Now he looked at me, eyebrow raised. "Are you kidding?"

"No. So I obviously had to stay with her. She wanted me to go with her to get the test and—"

"Fuck. Does she know whose it is?"

I had asked the same thing, but Jonah sounded more amused than sympathetic, and that rubbed me the wrong way. "Obviously, it's Kyle's. It's not like she sleeps around."

He snorted. "It's not? Right."

"What is that supposed to mean?"

He smirked. "It means that your friend is a whore. She's had her legs open for half of D-Phi. She's a running joke among my brothers. Ben needs to reel her in."

I stared at him, speechless, my face heating with both indignation and embarrassment for Penny. "But she's not. She's..."

He let out a bark of a laugh. "Yeah. Right. Sure. Where are we going here?"

I blinked and looked around. Even though we were stopped at a light, it felt like we were driving straight off a cliff. Did all of the D Phi brothers really talk about Penny like that? When I asked him what they'd thought about me, he'd said they were no one to him. Their opinion didn't matter. But apparently, if he was listening to them, it did. Now, I felt even worse for Penny. If she really was just a joke to all of them, Kyle was not going to be kind to her during that phone call. "Uh..."

The light turned green, and the car lurched forward. "Great idea," he quipped. "Let's get something to eat. You want burgers?"

I nodded numbly and was quiet for the rest of the ride to Burger

King. That saintly image that I'd had of him, being a fine, upstanding man and good dad, felt tarnished. Good guys didn't call girls whores. Penny had been really nice to him, too, on the few times they'd interacted. He knew she was my best friend. Why did he hate her so much? What had she done? Was it just because she'd slept with Kyle and other brothers in the fraternity?

He must've sensed I was upset because when we pulled into the lot and cut the engine, he turned to me and tugged playfully at my hair. "Hey. You okay?"

I nodded and forced a smile. "Yeah. Just... Penny's my best friend."

"Yeah, I get it," he said with a shrug. "You're such a great girl, wanting to take care of her. But you've gotta admit it. She's a bad influence on you."

I was speechless. An influence? No, she wasn't. She was my friend.

"Really. How hard was it to have the guy wear a condom, right?"

"I think she did. She was as shocked as—"

"That might be what she said, in hindsight. But does she know half of what she's doing when she's drunk off her ass like that?" he asked, giving me a condescending look. "I see it all the time, Ava. Your friend was so blitzed one night; she probably could've fucked half the house and not even realized it."

I blinked, trying to remember what night that was. Yes, Penny liked to drink and have fun, but she'd driven us there since she was the only one with a license. She'd never been too drunk to drive. At least, I didn't think so.

He was staring at me in the darkness, his eyes full of concern. "I'm just looking out for you. It's not okay to act like that. I don't want you to follow her example and get hurt."

"I don't follow her," I said weakly because that was a lie. I had been following her that first night at D-Phi.

"You shouldn't. It's not good for you. You're too sweet, and this world will corrupt you if you don't have someone to look out for you. Stick with me, kid."

I wanted to protest, but he was right. Penny had almost convinced me to throw caution to the wind and act the same way she'd been acting. And now look at her. Pregnant, alone. I probably shouldn't have been following her example.

And I always melted a little inside whenever he called me *kid*. Like it was just him and me against the world, he really wanted me safe, and I appreciated that. "I will," I said, my smile turning genuine.

"Good," he said, leaning in to give me a real kiss this time.

I still felt a little bad about Penny when he wrapped his arm around me and led me inside. But eventually, Jonah started telling me about his day, and I stopped thinking about her at all.

Chapter Seventeen

I woke up the following morning, knowing I'd forgotten something.

It hit me as I trudged to the shower to get ready for school. I was thinking about all the things I had to do that I'd rather not—an English essay on *Things Fall Apart,* cleaning my disaster of a bedroom, figuring out what colleges to apply to this weekend so I could finally get my dad off my back—when it hit me.

I'd never called Penny.

I rushed back to my room and sent her a quick *How are you doing?* so I wouldn't feel like the worst friend in the world when I saw her later that day at lunch. But I was the worst friend in the world. I fully knew that. She was going through a huge, life-altering crisis... and I just forgot?

But the talk I'd had with Jonah had set something off in me. Originally, I'd thought he was being heartless, but the more we talked about it, the more I realized he had a point. It wasn't as if she'd been afflicted with a disease she had no control over. Penny *had* brought this on herself. How many times had we sat through safe sex lectures at Wood Wil? Did she really think that drinking and sleeping with a bunch of different guys was going to turn out well for her?

The truth was, personal responsibility was a thing, and she'd screwed up. I had enough on my own plate without taking on her worries as my own. I could be there for her to a point, but she was the one who needed to face the consequences, whatever they were. Not me.

What mattered most in my own life was my relationship with Jonah. That was most important. And I could be there for my best friend, but not so much that I jeopardized things with my boyfriend. That only made sense.

I took the phone into the bathroom as I started the water in my shower. Steam had just begun to fill the air when Penny responded: *Fine. Would you come with me today after school?*

Guess she'd made an appointment at the clinic. That was good. I'd told Jonah that I'd go with her, and he said that was fine. He'd encouraged it, actually. But after that? I had to make sure boundaries were in place, so I didn't let her tragedy bring me down, too. That's all he was saying. I typed in: *Absolutely.*

When I got to lunch later that day, it was almost as if everything was normal. Penny had gone last night to get her hair done, this new style with chunky bangs and a fringe that framed her face. She looked happy and couldn't stop talking about how many compliments she'd gotten. Sara was trying to urge Penny to arrange another get-together with her hot neighbors again, but Penny was being noncommittal. "I don't know. It was only fun when we were able to swim in their pool. Now it's too cold."

Not to mention that soon she's going to have a bump, I thought, wondering when that actually happened. My knowledge of pregnancy was pretty spotty.

"But they were so hot for us!" Sara whined. "Come on. Just once more. Besides, that pool was heated!"

Penny glanced at me before shrugging. As they went on, it struck me that though I didn't know much about the hot neighbors, Penny hadn't told Sara the *big* secret, the one I knew.

Sara looked at me. "You should come the next time we get together," she said with a grin. "In case things with Jonah don't work out. Will might be a little chunky, but he's cute."

Will was the third guy, the one neither of them was interested in. "Thanks, but pass," I said, secure in the knowledge that I had everything I wanted with Jonah.

She shrugged and then said, "You seeing Jonah after school again?"

I looked at Penny and lied. "Yeah. Probably." I had to lie because if I said Penny and I were going anywhere together, she'd want to come along.

"What are you doing?" Sara asked Penny.

Penny said, "I have a lot of homework," which was a terrible excuse because she never let homework get in the way of fun. Penny was a solid C student and never aspired to do any better. I winced at the incredulous look Sara gave her in return, but thankfully, she let it drop.

After the last bell, Penny and I waited in the ladies' room until we made sure Sara was gone, and then we headed off to Vernon together. When we got to the clinic, I was a little surprised. It was in a one-story brick office building, and there were no signs on the front. But the moment we walked in, a woman came over to us with a welcoming smile. "Which one of you is Penelope?"

I winced on Penny's behalf because I knew how much she hated the name Penelope. But Penny had other things on her mind. She raised her hand weakly.

"Come with me, Dear," she said, wrapping an arm around her. She looked at me. "You may wait out here, please."

The waiting room was empty. I navigated to the mauve plastic chairs and sat down next to a rack of brochures for all kinds of health issues. I noticed one for safe sex and another for birth control, and without thinking, I covertly grabbed them. As I was about to tuck them into my bag, I thought about the heart attack my mother would have if she found them while cleaning my room. I quickly shoved them back into the plastic holder. Better to get the info online.

I waited there for about half an hour, getting more and more nervous that someone we knew might come in. But nobody did. The only person who came in was the mailman, delivering a pile of packages to the reception desk. He didn't even look at me.

Jonah texted at around four, asking how things were going. Just as I was about to text him back, the door opened, and Penny came out. She smiled at me. "You ready?"

I grabbed my bag. "Uh, sure."

She didn't say anything as I followed her out to the car or on the first few minutes of the ride home. Finally, I decided I had to know, even if she wasn't willing to tell me. "So? What did they say?"

"I'm about eight weeks along," she said, her voice emotionless.

I started thinking back to figure out when it happened, landing in mid-September, just when we'd gone to D-Phi for the first time and I met Jonah.

But Penny was thinking in a completely opposite direction. "That means my due date will be around graduation."

"Wait..." I said, hardly believing what I was about to say. "You're going to keep it?"

She let out a little huff. "Of course. I'm a Christian."

Strangely, I didn't know that. In all the years I'd known Penny, not once had she ever canceled weekend plans because she had to go to church. "Oh, but... how?"

"It's going to be fine," she said to me with a decisive nod. "First, I have to tell Kyle."

My stomach sank. "So you didn't tell Kyle about it yet?"

"No. I wanted to be sure first. They took blood and did an ultrasound. This little nugget's totally healthy. I heard the heartbeat!" She patted her stomach. "Anyway, after I tell him, we can tell our parents. Together."

As usual, Penny had it all planned. And she always seemed totally confident in her plan, which always made me think there was no way it could fail. But after hearing what Jonah had said about her and the guys at D-Phi, I wasn't so sure. And I'd never told her that I'd seen Kyle hooking up with another girl, either.

There was no way I could tell her those things now, so I just said, "That's great that you have a plan. What about college?"

She smiled. "College is no problem. If I have the baby at graduation, I can drop it off with my parents while I go to Icana. Of course, I'll go to the same school as Kyle, and we can get an apartment together. They have off-campus apartments for married students. I looked into it last night."

"You—" I began but bit back the rest of the sentence. *You think Kyle is going to marry you?* The last time I'd seen Kyle, he hadn't looked like he was ready to settle down. Far from it. Yes, I'd been having the same fantasies about Jonah and I having a future together, but Jonah was different. "Oh."

"I know, I know. He doesn't look like a fatherly type. But leave it to a wake-up call like this to really smack some sense into a guy," she said with a toss of her hair. "He'll fall in line. If he doesn't, *I'll* smack the sense into him."

She was on a tear. When she got like this, I knew better than to argue with her. Even though I had doubts, I nodded. "That's good."

She dropped me off at my house and thanked me for coming with her, and I told her to let me know how it went. I really didn't want to know, though, because I knew she was going to be let down. She was operating without a safety net, and I could just see her wobbling, about to fall. But there was nothing I could do.

That's how much I'd already come to value Jonah's opinion. Even then, it didn't matter what anyone else told me. In my mind, Jonah was always right.

Chapter Eighteen

"I'm going, Mom," I called from the living room. It was the weekend before Thanksgiving, and D-Phi was having a big party. I was excited—and a little nervous— to see him. We'd been dancing around the topic of sex for a long time, and I knew that I couldn't hold him off much longer.

"Honey, remember to be home by one like we agreed."

"Got it," I said, making sure I had my lip gloss in my purse. Since the last time I'd come home late, I told her that midnight was too restrictive because the party was just getting started by that time. At first, they'd argued, but then I told them that in another few months, I would be away at college myself. After a little back-and-forth, she'd agreed with me that since I hadn't come home drunk and I'd been getting good grades at school, they'd extend my curfew to one.

"Also, I'd really prefer it if you didn't drink while you're underage, but I understand there will be college kids there, so please just be responsible."

"Okay, mom."

I felt like I had made progress with her. *We* had made progress. She had gotten to know Jonah better, and so she now trusted us. I almost felt like an adult.

"You look gorgeous," he said to me as I slid into the front seat of his car. That was his usual greeting, and it never got old. I was dressed a lot more casually than I'd been for the first two parties because I realized by now that no one dressed up. I knew my clothes would end up reeking of beer and sweat by the end of the night anyway.

But he looked me over as if I was dressed to the nines. When he looked at me like that, I felt tingles down to the tips of my toes. "Thank you," I said, entwining my fingers with his as we drove to the Icana campus.

"I forgot to tell you, I have to do pledge duty tonight," he said with a groan.

"Oh," I said, disappointment threatening to cloud over. But that was okay, I decided. I'd spent a lot of time thinking about the last party, and I'd overreacted. I had been uncomfortable for no reason. I wasn't some random high school girl. I was a brother's girlfriend. I *belonged* there.

"If you don't want to mingle, you can hang out in my room if you want?" he suggested. He must've been thinking of the last time when I'd freaked out, awkwardly searching from room to room, looking for him.

"No. No, it's fine." I wished he'd introduced me to more people, but I could handle this. It was only for a few hours, anyway.

When we got to the party, it wasn't too crazy. I figured it was because it was still early, but then Jonah told me that a lot of the brothers had gone home for the holiday already, and it would be pretty chill.

When I walked through the door, I saw Penny coming down the stairs. I wondered if she'd talked to Kyle yet. I really hadn't seen her much since we went to the clinic. Only during lunches, and we couldn't discuss her situation with Sara there, and she was surrounded by half the senior class. "Hey, is Kyle here?"

Jonah shrugged. "I think he went home for the break."

He handed me a beer, gave me a kiss and said, "Don't get into too much trouble," before he took off for the basement to babysit the pledges.

"Have you talked to him yet?" I asked Penny as she reached

for her coat.

"Why do you think I'm here?" She snapped.

I could tell she didn't want to talk about it, at least not here. But she was already almost three months along, and I thought she would have told him by now.

"I just thought you would've told him in a... you know? A more private setting." I said, looking around at the crowd in the living room and the stranglers passing by us.

Penny sighed and for a moment, a look of defeat flashed across her face. "I thought this was something I should tell him in person, and I figured I'd have a better chance of seeing him here since he hasn't answered my calls and won't text me back."

At that moment, I felt so alone for Penny. She had this grand plan of working it out with Kyle and being parents of the year, but in reality, he wouldn't even speak to her.

"I'm sorry, Pen..." I started to say, but she cut me off.

"It's whatever. I'll tell him the next time I see him. Enjoy the party." Penny slipped out the door. I tried to remember what Jonah had said; these are the consequences of her own actions, and she has to face them herself.

I went to the kitchen, trying to distract myself from feeling sad for Penny. It was packed, so I stood and watched the beer pong game, figuring Jonah would find me when he was ready. I still didn't quite understand the game, but I started catching on the longer I watched. I drained my beer and was just about to get another one when a guy with spiky blonde hair grinned at me and held up the ball. "Want to play?"

Was he a brother? I'd never seen him before. I looked behind me, thinking he must've been talking to someone else. But there was no one else there. "Oh, no. I'm just watching. I don't know how to play anyway."

The corner of his mouth quirked up in a smile. "Are you kidding me? Everyone knows how to play!"

"Well, I've never played before, so I guess I'm not everybody," I said with a bit of sarcasm in my voice, surprising myself. It must've been the beer or Jonah, but I never used to be able to talk to guys, much less a cute college boy.

"No, you definitely aren't just anyone," this guy said with a wink. Was he flirting with me? From the way he looked me up and down, his eyes catching on my cleavage, I thought so. "I'll just have to teach you then. It's not hard."

He motioned the other brothers to move aside, clearing a path for me. I took another glance around and, when I didn't see Jonah, moved over to the counter next to him. As he showed me how to hold the ball to get the best angle for throwing, I thought about how Penny had done this, that first party. I'd been so jealous of her for fitting in so effortlessly.

Now, I was the one the girls were jealous of. I could sense them standing around the table, watching me. Everyone was. I'd never been in the spotlight before, not like Penny. I kind of liked it.

After I told him I understood, he gave me the plastic ball to try on my own. I attempted to get the ball in the cup, but it was harder than it looked. Embarrassingly, I missed three times in a row. Around me, a couple of girls snickered.

"It's okay. You'll get the hang of it. Let me help you," the guy said as he placed the ball in my hand and got behind me. He wrapped his hand around mine and helped me throw the ball so that it popped in. Everyone cheered.

"What're you doing?"

Suddenly, Jonah was standing right next to us, eyeing the guy's hand, which was wrapped around mine. Everyone else was having a good time, but he looked bothered.

"This guy was just showing me how to play beer pong," I said as I realized what Jonah might be thinking.

The guy, realizing that he was in the middle of something, let go of my hand and backed away. "Sorry, Jo. She yours?"

"Uh-huh," he said, grabbing my hand and yanking me out to the hallway, where it was less crowded. "Having fun?"

"I guess. At least that guy was talking to me. Otherwise, I'd feel just as lonely as that last party I went to," I said, pouting. "Are you done with pledge—"

Before I could finish the sentence, the back of Jonah's hand hit the side of my face. Stunned, I reached for my cheek. It didn't hurt exactly. I was too shocked to register the pain. I just stared at him, eyes wide, afraid to say anything else.

His eyes were cold. "You shouldn't talk to me that way, Ava. I came here to have a good time, and finding you with that guy and having you talk to me like that is *not* a good time. Good girlfriends don't get impatient and start flirting with other guys. Good girlfriends don't make their boyfriends feel like shit."

"Oh." I tasted blood in my mouth and wondered if my cheek was going to swell. The words tumbled out of my mouth. "I didn't know. I mean... Sorry."

He smiled uneasily. "Come on. Let's go dance."

Jonah tightly grabbed my wrist and walked me through the back door. I knew it was bad, but I'd already started rationalizing it. After all, he had been drinking, and sometimes people could be aggressive when they were drunk. And he always said that dealing with the pledges and all this "fraternity bullshit" got on his nerves. His grip didn't loosen on my hand as he pulled me out onto the dance floor. As he pulled me against him, I told myself not to do anything that would upset or embarrass him any further.

We would just have fun. I tried to get lost in the music, but when I closed my eyes, I kept seeing the way he'd looked at me. It was like I disgusted him, and I hated that.

I'd be good. No, not just good. I'd be the *perfect* girlfriend.

Jonah leaned forward and kissed me. He slid his tongue into my parted lips and ran his hands down my sides, cupping my butt. I felt his erection press against me.

It only felt like a few seconds. Maybe it was longer. But a moment later, he started pulling me toward the main staircase. I let him, because of that earlier promise to myself that I'd try not to make him angry. It was only when we were halfway up the grand, sweeping staircase, its blood-red carpet dotted with lint and unrecognizable dark stains, that it started to dawn on me.

Good girlfriends don't make their boyfriends feel like shit. If I said no to him again, he'd feel like shit.

If I let him do what he wanted, I would not be leaving here a virgin.

At that, the beer in my gut started to swirl, and I began to feel sick. Like a snowball that had been pushed down a hill, I was in freefall, with no way of stopping myself.

"Uh, Jonah," I began as we neared his room at the end of the hall.

But one of his brothers had stopped him. "You got it?"

"Yeah, yeah," he said. "One second."

He guided me to his room. As a senior, he had a single, and it was a pretty big space, with windows overlooking fraternity row. I'd been in there once before, during the day, but suddenly, it seemed more sinister now. I didn't know why. He had a full bed that took up most of the room, and like last time, there was a rumpled ball of sheets in the center. There were crates stuffed in his closet, filled with the things he was trying to sell online—everything from video games to collectibles. His desk was a mess of books except for a line of empty liquor bottles, and he had an overflowing collapsible hamper hooked to the back of the door.

He swept in, opened the drawer, and pulled out what looked like an oversized pencil case. "One second. Business calls." He smirked. "Make yourself at home."

I perched on the very edge of the bed, shivering, and not just because it was a lot colder upstairs than at the party. He clearly did well with his business because he was always talking about getting a new car and moving to the city when he graduated. But I hadn't known he conducted business with his brothers. What could he possibly be selling to them from that tiny pouch?

That sick feeling intensified as I sat there, hugging myself and mulling over the possibilities. Only one thing made sense.

Was I dating a drug dealer?

Okay, no. That was impossible. Jonah was sweet, smart, and going places. He was about to graduate from college. All my friends said he was the perfect boyfriend. And the perfect boyfriend wouldn't ruin his life by doing something illegal, right?

Right.

Except that he'd also slapped me, and the perfect boyfriend probably wouldn't do that, either.

Of course, I had been acting like a brat. I shouldn't have been flirting with that guy in Jonah's house. That was wrong.

When Jonah returned, he shoved the pouch back into a drawer and reached for me. "So, where were we?"

I jumped up suddenly, checking my phone. "Actually. I have to go. I have curfew at eleven."

He frowned. "Eleven?"

"Well, yeah. I failed a test, and they're tightening the leash, I guess." I rolled my eyes, mock annoyed.

"Oh." He checked his phone. "Shit. All right. We can get

together tomorrow."

"Well, not tomorrow night. I have this thing with the girls," I admitted softly.

I expected he'd complain about that, maybe even slap me again, but I guess he must've been feeling guilty about the slap because he didn't argue at all.

He just took me home and gave me a sweet kiss before I got out of the car. As I was about to go, he said, "We're okay, right?"

I stared at him, unsure if he meant what I was thinking he meant. As much as I'd wanted to put it behind us, that slap had changed things. Now more than ever, I felt like I was walking a tightrope around him. My answer reflected that. "Yeah."

"Good. Remember that girlfriend I talked about?? The reason I got so upset was because she cheated on me. I don't want to be the fool again. You understand that, right, Ava?"

I nodded. That made sense. He'd been hurt before. "I'll never hurt you, Jonah. I promise."

He smiled and cupped my cheek. "I believe that, Ava."

It was nothing more than a simple misunderstanding. Now that I knew about his past relationship, I'd be more careful not to flirt with other boys. By the time I got into bed, I'd forgotten all about it. After all, I told myself, everyone has their bad days, and that was ours. We'd emerged from it closer and with a deeper understanding of one another. That was the way relationships worked. Things would be just fine.

Chapter Nineteen

"Thank you again for being free tonight," I said to my two friends when they showed up at my front door.

"Of course! We haven't seen you in forever. A girl's day is long overdue!" Penny announced, throwing down her bag as I started to close the front door, noticing her mom speeding off down the street.

"Wait, what happened to your car, Pen?" I asked.

Penny and Sara looked at each other.

"The Beamer kind of got totaled," she whispered.

"Oh my gosh, Pen, what happened?"

"Remember when I texted you guys S.O.S.? Well, some jerk tried to cut me off, and I wasn't about to let that happen, so I went after him. And then he ran me right off the road. I crashed into a tree."

I *didn't* remember that. My first thought was about the baby, but I still wasn't sure if Sara had been filled in. As I stood there, confused at how out of the loop I was, I felt like the worst friend in the world. "Penny, oh my gosh, why didn't you tell me? Are you okay?"

"Yeah, it was like a week ago. I'm fine." Penny looked down at her hands, and Sara put a hand on her back.

"Luckily, she wasn't hurt. Unfortunately, we can't say the same about the car," Sara chimed in.

"That must've been when I was with Jonah. I'm so sorry, Penny. I wasn't paying attention to my phone."

"Yeah, well, you were busy. Sara came over after, so it was all good. I just don't have a car anymore, and my parents aren't getting me a new one. They want to teach me responsibility or something. So, now I have to get a job if I want a car." She made a face like *That's never going to happen.*

Penny looked fine physically, but she was clearly upset. I hadn't been there for her during the accident, and I hadn't talked to her at all about the pregnancy. Had she even spoken to Kyle? It had been weeks since she'd gone to the clinic, but I hadn't really followed up with her. That made me feel even worse.

"I'm sorry, Penny. I'm glad you're okay. And, hey, we're all together tonight, so let's have some fun."

Penny nodded. "Yeah, I know. We'll have a good time tonight."

"Still, it would've been nice if you had followed up or called Penny after you saw her S.O.S., Ava," Sara said.

Sara was right. I'd been too absorbed by other things. I'd seen the S.O.S. and just assumed it was something stupid, like who Penny saw holding hands in the hallway. If only I'd known, I would've dropped everything.

Before I could make the excuse, Penny said, "So, do we want to do dinner first or face masks?"

"It's too early for dinner. Let's do the masks first," Sara said.

"Ugh, okay, but I'm hungry, so I'm getting a snack first." Penny pulled some Cheez-Its out of the cabinet and shoved her hand in. "When are you seeing Jonah this weekend?" Penny asked with a mouth half full of orange dust.

I sighed. "I don't know yet. Maybe tomorrow. He asked me to hang out tonight, but I told him I already had plans with you guys. Besides, we already hung out last night."

"Oh, so you just wanted to switch it up because he's smothering you?" Sara said, stealing some Cheez-Its from Penny's hand.

"What happened? Was the sex bad?" Penny asked, pinning me

with her gaze.

"No... we haven't done that yet," I said, looking down.

"Really?" they asked in unison. Penny added, "I thought for sure you'd have given up the goods by now. Jonah's so hot and perfect."

I nodded. "I know. I don't know what's wrong with me. I just want it to be really special, and a frat bedroom doesn't feel special."

Penny laughed. "If you build it up in your head to be some Disney fairy tale, you're going to be disappointed."

I thought about last night and the slap. "Sometimes I wonder why he's even with me," I said, my voice small.

"Ava, you're amazing. Any guy would be lucky to have you as their girlfriend and Jonah knows that. He wouldn't be sticking around if he wasn't into you," Sara said, licking the orange dust from her fingers.

"But he's been with other girls, and I don't know anything."

"What do you mean, 'been with?'" Penny asked.

"I mean, he had a girlfriend before me. When he was in high school, he said they slept together, and she was his first everything."

"Good! That's a good thing. That means he knows what he's doing, and it's going to be so much better for you for your first time, Ava!" Penny nodded.

"But I have no idea what I'm doing!"

"Well, if you want, I can teach you how to give killer blowjobs." Penny smirked, looking around. "Give me a banana."

"Ugh, Penny, please, no one's going to have an appetite for dinner if you talk about giving head," Sara piped up.

"Every guy wants a blow job whether they say it or not. If Ava's so worried about keeping him interested, she can have a few tricks up her sleeve," Penny said with a wink in my direction.

"Can we start doing masks or what?" Sara asked as she got up and made her way to the bathroom.

Penny looked at me as if to ask, *What's wrong with her?* I shrugged. Penny started making obscene hand gestures. "All you need to do is just take it and—"

"Ugh, really?" Sara was back, a pile of masks in her hands.

"That is what I'm saying! I'm sure other college girls have done this before and would be way better at it than me," I whined as Penny continued to make hand gestures.

"God, Ava, enough already," Sara muttered, sounding hurt. "Jonah is lucky to have you, okay? You have nothing to worry about. If he wanted to be with someone just to have good sex, he would find someone else. You'll be fine. Now, can we stop talking about Jonah for like 10 minutes?"

I guess I was being *that* friend. The annoying one who couldn't stop talking about her boyfriend. Besides, I'd neglected them for him, and now all I was doing was talking about him. Even though I wanted to get more advice from Penny, I said, "Sorry. Okay, so who wants the rehydrating mask, and who wants the charcoal one?"

Penny said she wanted the hydrating mask, so I took the charcoal one, and Sara took the green tea mask for herself.

"Okay, I want to take this necklace off before I get charcoal on it," I asked as I started to loosen the necklace off my neck.

"Wait—is that the necklace Jonah gave to you?" Sara asked.

"Oh, ah. Yeah." I said, not one minute after I pledged not to mention Jonah for the rest of the night. "I'll just take it off, and we can get started on our girl's night."

"Wow," Penny said. "Jewelry. Big step."

"You are so lucky," Sara said. She picked the pendant up off my palm and looked at it closely. "It's gorgeous. He must really like you."

"No, he *loves* her," Penny said, drawing the word out in a mocking tone.

"Stop, he just wanted me to know how he feels about me," I said. "That's all."

For the rest of the night, I tried to have fun. But it just paled in comparison to whatever I'd be doing with Jonah. They didn't want me talking about him non-stop, and as much as I understood that, I couldn't think of anything interesting to talk about that didn't involve him. All the gossip about high school bored me now. I found my mind wandering and wishing the night would be over so that I could text Jonah.

When our girls' night was over, I rushed to my phone, expecting to have a text from Jonah. I'd texted him before, telling him I missed him.

But there was nothing.

Very odd. When I went to bed, I decided he was probably out with his friends. He was allowed to spend time with his friends, just like I was.

But then I started thinking about the time I'd seen Kyle with that other girl. What if they were having a party, and Jonah had met another girl? What if she was cooler than me, and he'd forgotten all about me?

No, that was silly. He'd gotten completely bent out of shape over me talking to another guy. It worked both ways. If he was that serious about us being faithful to one another, I had nothing to worry about when it came to him talking to another girl.

Even so, I barely slept at all that night. When I woke up, I checked my phone first thing.

Still no text from Jonah. He was probably still sleeping but it was unlike him to not respond for so long. I sent another text just to say good morning. But there was nothing.

Stop it, Ava. Give him some space. Like the girls said, it's healthy to be apart sometimes.

I spent the whole day Netflix-binging and obsessively checking my phone between shows. Eventually, my mom called down to me in the living room.

"Ava, honey, did you hear me? Dinners on the table," she said.

That snapped me out of my binging trance. I breathed in the smell of fresh baked mac and cheese and got up off the couch. Before I made my way to the dining room, I checked my phone again. Still no messages from Jonah.

Now, I was really worried. No, we didn't have plans that night, but we usually spent at least some time together on the weekends. It was unlike Jonah not to text me for a few hours, let alone a whole day. I shot him another text just to check in and decided I'd call after dinner if I needed to.

My mom had made pot roast along with the mac and cheese I'd smelled earlier. My parents were already sitting at the table, waiting for me. "Did you have fun with your friends last night, kiddo?" my dad asked.

I nodded. "It was nice."

"It must've been. You haven't seen them in a while, right, honey?" my mother said, and for some reason, it felt like an accusation.

I clenched my fists under the table and nodded. It was not my fault. Or maybe it was. Who cared? Who cared if I found Jonah and being with him far more interesting than the people from my old life? I was allowed to hang out with whomever I wanted.

"It's nice to have such good friends," my mother said again. "They're special."

My parents were probably right, but it didn't feel that way. My *friends* didn't understand me anymore. Neither did my parents. I have new priorities now. Only Jonah seemed to understand that.

Jonah, who was totally MIA. Why wasn't he texting me back?

"Where's Jonah tonight?" Her dad asked suddenly.

"I don't know. I thought he'd come over, but I haven't heard from him," I muttered without looking up from my plate.

"Did you have plans?"

"No, we didn't, but we usually see each other on the weekends."

"Honey, I'm sure he has other things in his life than you. It's okay if you don't spend every weekend together," my father continued as my pulse continued to rise.

"I *know*," I spat out, dropping my fork. "May I be excused?"

My mother's brow knitted. "But honey, you haven't—"

"I'm not hungry," I said and got up anyway, rushing off to my bedroom. I closed the door, collapsed on the bed, and unlocked my phone to call Jonah.

"Look who finally called. It's nice to hear from you," was Jonah's answer.

Now, I was confused. Hadn't I been texting all this time? "Hey. What're you up to?"

"Right now, I'm just about to play basketball with the boys."

"Oh, okay, so you're not coming over this weekend then?"

"I wasn't planning on it. Did we have plans?"

"No, I just thought you'd want to hang out, that's all."

"You made it obvious the other day you didn't want to hang out. I mean, c'mon Ava, asking to leave the party early? And 'the girls want to do face masks.' Find a better excuse next time," he said with a calm hostility in his voice.

He was angry at me. He felt played. That was why he was

giving me the silent treatment? But now *I* feel played. "It wasn't a cover; I *did* do face masks with the girls."

He snorted. "Yeah. All I know is that I thought we had a special connection, and you made it clear you didn't have time for me this weekend. Do you not feel the same way?"

I blinked as I fingered the pendant he'd given me. It was a sweet gesture, made to show me how much he cared. But what had I done to show him *I* cared? Nothing. I hadn't thought about the possibility that he could be hurt by my wanting to leave so early Friday night. Once again, I'd been too focused on myself and the billions of other insecurities I harbored to think about how Jonah was feeling.

"Of course, I feel a connection with you. I care about you, Jonah. I didn't mean to upset you, and I wanted to see you tonight. I wish you had answered my texts earlier today so we could have planned something."

"Well, I was busy. I was only free last night." His voice had an edge to it.

"Okay, I understand. I didn't realize that. If you had told me—"

"You told me you had something with your friends that was more important." He spoke over me. "It's whatever, Ava. Really."

He sounded so cold; it made me shiver. "I didn't mean to upset you."

"Whatever. It's fine. Hey, I've got to go," he said with so much aloofness I wanted to jump through the phone and grab hold of him. It felt like he was blowing me off.

Desperation crept into my voice. "Okay... then will I see you before Thanksgiving?"

"Probably not. I've got some stuff to do. And a family thing on Thursday."

A family thing. Of course, I did too. It was Thanksgiving, after all. My grandparents would all be over, and we'd have the whole traditional feast, which was the same thing I'd had since I was a baby. But my spirits really fizzled when I imagined not seeing him for that long. "Oh. Okay."

"Wait. You want to come with me?"

My breath caught. A second ago, I'd been worried that his feelings for me were cooling off. Now, he wanted to bring me to his family's Thanksgiving celebration? I hadn't met his parents yet, but we talked about it. This would be a huge step forward in our relationship.

I jumped at the offer. "Yes. I'd love to!"

"Cool," he said, and it was only after I hung up that I realized my parents were not going to be happy about me missing Thanksgiving at home.

I shrugged those worries off. Yes, I always liked seeing our family during the holidays. But this was an important milestone in my relationship with Jonah, and our holiday feast was always the same thing every year. My family would get over it. I could make it up to them on Christmas.

Chapter Twenty

"Thanks, Mom, again, for letting me go to Jonah's for dinner," I said to my mom as she pulled a sweet potato pie out of the oven.

She inhaled the pie and set it on the stove to cool. "Well, you're going to be missing this."

I smiled, my heart twisting a little. As much as I'd tried to convince myself that all of our Thanksgiving traditions were goofy and I wouldn't care about them, part of me felt sad for all that I'd miss. I'd even miss my grandparents, constantly asking me about my future and what college I was going to. But I kept reminding mom—and myself—that I'd be there for Christmas and bring Jonah, too. It was exciting and a little scary thinking about introducing him to my whole family... but first, I had other things on my mind.

First, I had to worry about making a good impression with *his* family.

That's why it didn't even faze me that I was going to be missing mom's famous pie—my stomach was already in knots as it was. I probably wouldn't even be able to eat more than a few mouthfuls of turkey.

For the thousandth time that day, I checked my reflection— this time in the glass of the pantry door. I was wearing an oversized sweater, denim skirt, and boots, an outfit I'd taken great care of selecting. I wanted to make a good impression.

"I'm glad you and Jonah are getting along so well," my mom said as she buzzed around the kitchen. "And that he wants you to meet his family. You know, it's very important to get along with your partner's family. As you get older, you'll be seeing them for holidays and birthdays and sometimes more than that. Don't you like how often you get to see your grandmother?"

I nodded. "Yeah, I love seeing nanna."

"Well, you probably wouldn't see her as much if I didn't get along with your father's family. In fact, we may not have even gotten married if I didn't like his family," she said, turning on the sink.

I thought about how Penny had seemed so sure that she was going to get married to Kyle because she was having his baby. Though I'd had fantasies about doing that with Jonah, I couldn't actually see myself doing anything like that. Not for a long time. "Mom, please, I'm not getting married anytime soon."

"I'm just saying it's a big step, honey. I'm happy to support you, but just be careful and kind to everyone. We're all going to miss you tonight."

"I get it." The doorbell rang. "I'll be back later, mom."

"I'll save you some of Aunt Moira's pecan roll that you like."

"Thanks, mom. I love you," I said as I kissed her cheek.

"Love you back," she called after me as I made my way to the front door.

Before I knew it, we were pulling up to Jonah's house. I'd never seen Jonah's house before. Since his father was a doctor, I'd been expecting something very modern and upscale, but his house was an old-style, bi-level house with green shingles and white shutters. Not an imposing mansion, but not a little shack, either. Quaint. Cute. I could see a young Jonah growing up there.

The front door was open, and some people were making their way into the house, carrying trays of food. It reminded me of my family's Thanksgiving and how everyone brought a side dish.

"Everyone is basically here. I don't think my cousin who's in Iowa is coming, but otherwise, everyone else should be here," he said once we'd found a parking space at the curb.

I followed Jonah out of the car, but it wasn't until I hit the sidewalk that I *really* started to feel nervous. What if they didn't like me? What if I didn't fit in or have anything witty to say?

Jonah grabbed my hand as we crossed the street, which made me feel better.

The first room was a tiny foyer with a coat rack covered in guests' coats and mismatched shoes everywhere. We climbed a staircase into a living room, and I held my breath, thinking that they'd all be looking at me.

But that's not what happened. The room was packed with men drinking beer and intently watching a football game. One man was feeding a baby in his lap with a bottle. And they were shouting. *Loudly.* Since I wasn't a big sports fan, I couldn't tell if they were shouting at the screen or at each other. I was just happy they weren't staring at me.

Jonah cleared his throat. "Hey. Guys. This is Ava. My girlfriend."

Eyes gradually shifted to me, and they all started shouting at us, but in a good way. "*Ayyyy!*" one of them said. A guy with graying hair and a Steelers jersey said, "She's too pretty for you." The guy with the baby said to me, "How'd he trick you into coming to this madhouse?"

I laughed as Jonah introduced them. "This is my dad," he said as a man with curly dark hair stood up and offered me his hand. He had Jonah's dark eyes and thick-rimmed glasses.

"A pleasure, Ava!" he said brightly.

"Nice to meet you, Dr. Manzano," I said, trying to be polite.

"Please, call me John!" He squeezed my hand tightly and looked at his son. "She's cute as a button, Jo Jo."

I blushed, but I immediately felt at home by his warm greeting. I received waves from a couple of cousins. An uncle. A grandfather. I lost track and didn't remember a single name. Jonah's soft, warm breath on my ear made me feel close to him even though we were in a room full of people.

After that, Jonah pulled me into the kitchen, where all the women were gathered around a huge assortment of charcuterie, talking animatedly about something.

As soon as we walked into the room, they all turned toward me as if I was the newest thing to gossip about. I felt awkward again but pasted a bright smile on my face.

"I'm guessing you're all staring because Ava is so beautiful. Am I right?" Jonah said, popping an olive into his mouth.

"Oh, Ava. We have heard so much about you." A large lady with teased black hair wrapped her arm around me. She smelled of some strong perfume. "I'm Jonah's favorite Aunt Luci."

"You're my only Aunt Luci," he said with a grin, and she punched him playfully.

I laughed and then went through the introductions. The only ones I really remembered were Aunt Luci and his mom, who was thin and pretty and had Jonah's smile.

A loud, shrill timer went off, and Aunt Luci gasped before opening the oven to take the bird out. A couple of kids—more cousins— passed back and forth between the kitchen and living room, and Jonah stopped each one to introduce me. It was nice to see how sweet he was with the children. It was one thing to see him on campus, acting like the fraternity brother, but here, I got to see this whole other side of him.

His family clearly adored him, and why shouldn't they? He was amazing. Amazing, and he was choosing to spend time with me. I couldn't help but feel like the luckiest girl in the world.

The dining room table wasn't nearly big enough for everyone, so Jonah's family scattered out between the dining and living rooms. The biggest table, and the table we sat at, was the one in the dining room. I took a seat right next to Jonah, next to another aunt. The dinner went smoothly, and the conversation flowed well. There was talk of what sports the kids were playing now, who got a job promotion, who got a dog. I tried to keep up with it all, but I didn't know most of the people they were talking about. As happy as I was to listen and learn about all of Jonah's family, it was a little overwhelming. By the time dessert came out, I was exhausted and ready to go home.

Jonah must've sensed that because he didn't linger. Right after he finished his pie, he said, "Well, we've got to go."

Everyone made a fuss over his leaving, and they all said how nice it was to meet me. One of his uncles even hugged me and told me I was already part of the family. As we walked back to the car, I felt good, like I'd accomplished something important.

"It made me really happy that you came," Jonah said, holding my hand tight.

"They were all so nice. It wasn't hard to get along with everyone," I told him.

"I can tell they love you. I'm just grateful that you were able to come and make such a good impression. I'm lucky to have you, you know that?"

Jonah leaned down and gave me a kiss before opening the car door. The pure, unbridled happiness on his face and the softness of his kiss made me melt right into the passenger seat.

Then he reached down and pulled the seatbelt over me, strapping me into the car like I was his most precious possession. "I love you, too, Ava. You're so perfect for me."

My heart thudded to a stop. He loved me. He loved me. All my life, I'd imagined a boy saying those words to me. Not someone who was required to say those words, like a family member.

Someone I'd somehow made to love me. I felt like my heart was about to explode with love for him, so I blurted, "I love you, too, Jonah."

He kissed me again, just a short kiss, and tucked a lock of hair behind my ear. We grinned at each other, two people so deeply in love that nothing and no one else mattered.

I'm the luckiest girl in the world, I thought to myself all the way home.

Chapter Twenty-One

It had been the easiest two weeks since I spent Thanksgiving with Jonah's family. I must've made a good impression because ever since he'd wanted to spend every moment with me. When he wasn't with me, he was constantly texting and calling to let me know how much he missed me. He even started calling me during my lunch break to get an update on how my morning was going, so I began missing the lunch period. I'd text him when I got home from school to let him know I made it home safely and call him before going to bed so that he was the last thing I thought of before drifting off.

It was blissful, but all this time with Jonah meant that I barely saw Sara and Penny. When I was finally able to make some time for them for Christmas shopping on Saturday afternoon, I felt like I had so much to fill them in on.

"That is so sweet that he even introduced you to all his family!" Sara said after I told them about our Thanksgiving.

"I really felt like he was proud to have me there," I said.

"Of course, he was proud to show you off. You're hot, and guys love to show off their hot girlfriends," Penny said.

"Come on, Penny. We're in high school. Jonah's family is not thinking about how hot Ava is," Sara said.

"Yeah, they are. All those dirty old guys want to jump her, too. They just won't say it."

I scoffed. "They weren't dirty! His dad's a doctor! And his grandfather was like 90."

Penny refused to back down. "So?"

Sara glared at her. "Anyway, is he coming for Christmas then, since you met his family for Thanksgiving?"

"Yeah, so we're going to do Christmas Eve at our own houses since there's not much going on anyway, and then he'll be over to have dinner with my family on Christmas Day. He has younger cousins staying over, so he wants to help put cookies out for Santa and open presents with them in the morning."

"That's so sweet! He must be good with kids then," Sara said.

"Calm down. No one is having kids anytime soon," Penny said, to which I looked at her. It was a combination of Jonah's warning to me not to get too close to her drama and the touchiness of it all, but I was pretty in the dark about her pregnancy. The one time I'd managed to get her alone to ask how things were going, she'd simply said, *fine*, and changed the subject. I got the feeling she didn't want to talk about it, so I didn't.

"It's sweet. Are you nervous for him to meet your family?" Sara asked.

"No. I mean kind of. He's already met my parents, which is most important right? I'm excited, though, because most of my mom's family come to Christmas. You know my dad only has one sister, so Thanksgiving isn't as many people, but Christmas is a blast!"

"This is getting serious, Ava. I hope he gets along with your family as well as you got along with his," Sara said.

"I think he will. He seems to get along with everyone."

I felt my phone buzz and looked down to see Jonah was calling for the second time. I shot him a quick text to let him know I was still out shopping with the girls and that I'd give him a call later when I got home.

A few hours of shopping and a few mall pretzels later, we were exhausted. I was excited because I'd gotten Jonah a new wallet. His old one was falling apart. Not only did I want to get him something he would use, but I liked the idea that he'd think of me every time he used it. I'd even had it engraved with a special message: *My life has changed for the better with you in it—Ava.*

I smiled at that. It was the best way I could express the way I felt about him. Being with him made me feel on top of the world. I was nervous to confess my feelings with such a personal gift, but it was the truth. Besides, he'd expressed his feelings with the necklace, so it only made sense that I reciprocated.

When I got home, I went up to bed to wrap the presents, but the second I set everything up, I yawned. I reclined against the pillows and closed my eyes.

About a thousand years later, I woke up, blinking against the bright sun.

I jolted up in a panic. What time was it?

Grabbing for my phone, my heart seized up. Where was it?

I spread my arms out over the bed and didn't feel it anywhere. I checked the bedside table and lifted the covers before rolling out of bed and checking the floor.

Nope. It was nowhere to be found. When had I seen it last? I couldn't remember. The last time I'd had it was when Jonah had called me...

Oh, no. Jonah! I was supposed to call him back!

Frantic, I pulled the covers clear off the bed, checking everywhere in my room before confirming it wasn't there.

I rushed down the stairs and noticed the time on the clock on the fireplace mantle. It was afternoon! I'd never slept that long before. I checked everywhere, looking in the shopping bags I'd brought with me, searching my purse again and again. Then I asked my mom to call my phone.

"It must have fallen out of my pocket in Penny's mom's car," I said, picking up the landline to call Penny. I groaned and set it down. "I don't even know her number without my phone."

Mom came over and massaged my shoulder. "I was just on the way to the food store. Just relax, and I'll stop by Penny's on my way home. I'll be going right past it."

I smiled. "Thanks, Mom."

I started to run up the stairs, but my mother called to me. "Honey. Did you fill out your college applications yet?"

I froze, my stomach sinking. Most of my friends at school had already applied. "Almost. I just have one more section to do."

Conveniently, I left out that it was the biggest section—the essay. The thought of it made me want to cry. I'd do it eventually.

When I reached the top stairs, I turned to see her giving me a disapproving look. "Just get them done."

I would, but the truth was, it didn't feel that important anymore. Jonah and I had talked and agreed that Icana made the most sense since I'd be able to stay around Seagreen and commute and see him every day. And anyone could get into Icana. They had rolling admission, so I was in no rush.

As I took a shower, I started thinking about how I could make Jonah's Christmas gift even better. I'd just had a whole bunch of senior photos taken—I could add a picture of myself. After I changed, I went through my envelope and picked out the nicest one. Then I found some card stock paper, colored pens, stickers, and stencils and made him a nice homemade card. Once I wrapped the whole thing, it looked really good. I'd put a lot of thought into it because I wanted to show him how special he was to me.

As I was cleaning up the art supplies, a pen rolled off my bed and onto the floor. I got up and reached behind the nightstand to pick it up but noticed an object there.

My phone! It must've fallen behind the nightstand last night.

I shoved the nightstand aside and grabbed the phone, tapping the display, which stayed dark. Battery dead. I plugged it in and went to put the art supplies away. As I was shoving them into the drawer, my mom came inside with a bunch of groceries. "Oh, hon, I couldn't—"

"Don't worry, Mom. I found it," I said.

"Oh good! Where was it?"

"It was behind my dresser, and it's dead, so that's why it didn't ring."

"Well, I'm glad you found it and didn't lose it. Please try to keep better track of your phone, Ava. Those things are expensive to replace."

"I will, Mom. Thanks for helping me look for it earlier."

I went back to my room to see if my phone had charged enough to turn on. It lit up when I touched it, the home screen flooded with messages. I had over 20 messages and 4 missed calls from Jonah alone and a few more from my group chat with Sara and Penny.

I read through his messages. The messages from yesterday and this morning were asking me if I'd gotten home safe and if I was okay. As they went along, though, the messages got more serious. *Are you mad at me?* and *Did I do something wrong?*

The last message was so cold it made me shiver. *If you want your space, just tell me.*

It was exactly what I worried might happen. Quickly, I dialed his number to smooth things over. But when I called, the phone just rang and rang. I called three times in a row with no answer.

Then I texted him: *Sorry! I lost my phone! I just found it. All good.*

No response.

I spent the rest of the day wondering what he was up to. I sent him another text since I thought that we might get together that night, but he never responded. I went to sleep the following night with my phone right on my nightstand so I could be ready to grab it the second he called.

He never did. Not until Monday, when I was just about to leave class. My heart jumped when I got a text from him.

Come to the pick-up lot. I'm waiting for you.

My whole body jumped. He could've asked me to do anything at that moment, and I would've said yes.

But as I was getting my books from my locker at the end of the day, a feeling of nervous dread swept over me.

As I made my way to the lot, I read and re-read the message. His message wasn't nice or flirtatious. It was rather to the point. What if he was going to break up with me?

Jonah got out of his car as I neared. He didn't look particularly happy, but he didn't look upset either. He was wearing cargo pants with paint on them and a well-worn sweatshirt that hugged his muscles. Why did he look like he was in the middle of painting a house? He hadn't made an effort to look good—is this what guys wore when they broke up with you?

But as I got closer, Jonah opened his arms as I stepped up to him. Hesitantly, I let him fold me into a hug.

"That's it? I don't even get a real hug from my girlfriend I haven't seen all weekend?" he murmured.

I tried to squeeze him harder, but he pulled away.

"I missed you. I'm sorry again about what happened," I said to him.

He shrugged, aloof. "Okay. I just needed to see you and make sure everything was okay between us. I know what it's like to get blown off, and it felt a lot like what happened."

"Of course not! I just lost my phone after I got back from shopping with the girls. Then I found it under the bed." I rolled my eyes.

He studied me, suspicious. "Right."

"It's true! I really wanted to see you yesterday and missed talking to you. *Really*."

I reached for him, but he was stiff. He looked like he was trying to decide whether or not to believe me. "You really just lost your phone? There's nothing between us that needs to be fixed?"

"Nothing at all, Jonah. You make me incredibly happy. I was thinking about you all weekend and even got you the perfect Christmas present!"

"Oh, did you? I can't wait to see it." Jonah seemed to soften a little as he reached over to open the car door for me.

The ride home was quiet but reassuring. He held my hand, and I felt like things were getting back to normal. But then he pulled into a gas station. "I'm running on fumes. You don't mind, do you?"

I shook my head.

He got out to fill up the car. I sat there, scrolling through my phone, and happened to look down in the well by my feet and saw that little pouch that he'd had in his room. His business pouch.

I really wanted to open it up and look inside, but I knew he would be back at any moment. As I was about to check to see where he was, he bent down to look at me through the window. "I'm going to get a Coke. You want anything?"

I shook my head.

Watching in the rear-view mirror as he walked into the convenience store, I reached down and tugged on the zipper. The first thing I saw was a stack of cash. I riffled through them and realized that it was hundreds. But there was nothing else in there. Just a notepad.

Checking to make sure Jonah wasn't coming back, I pulled the notepad out to see if there was anything written on it, and my breath caught.

It was a prescription pad for Dr. John Manzano. His father.

I stared at it until it blurred in front of me, so in shock that I almost didn't see him coming out of the sliding doors with his Coke in hand. Quickly, I shoved the pad back into place and pulled on the zipper, then placed it back by my feet.

My mind reeled the whole way home. If he was forging prescriptions from his father, he could be in huge trouble. Was he on drugs, too? Was that his idea of a "successful business," dealing drugs to the people in his fraternity?

When we pulled up to my house, he said, "I can only stay a little while. Business calls."

Truthfully, I was glad. "Business?"

He nodded but didn't say more.

"What business?"

He shrugged. "You know."

I didn't know. I realized there was a lot about him that he was keeping from me and had no plans to tell me about. I pointed to the pouch. "What's in there?"

He grinned. "What, that? A shitload of cash. I've got to take it to the bank."

"Can I see?"

He reached down, opened it, and pulled out a stack of hundred-dollar bills, fanning it. "New wheels, here I come."

I think he wanted me to be impressed. But I just said, "What's that?" pointing to the pad.

He pulled it out and said, "Scratch paper. For notes."

I gave him an incredulous look. "It's a prescription pad from your dad's office. You're not using that to get drugs, are you?"

His smile fell. "Of course not." He opened the pouch and tipped it over. "You see any drugs in here?"

"No, but—"

Something like rage burned in his eyes, instantly making me wish I hadn't asked. "Who do you think I am? Are you insinuating I'm some kind of drug dealer?"

"Well..." Yes, I was. But I was clearly upsetting him, too.

He grabbed the pouch and shoved everything in, then threw it by my feet. "I'll see you."

After a few seconds, I realized he wanted me to get out of the car. "I thought you were going to come in and hang out."

"No, I have some things to do. I just wanted to see you and make sure we were okay."

Suddenly, things didn't feel like they were okay. "What do you need to do? Maybe you can do it later tonight?"

"It's just some business stuff that needs to get done now. I'll see you this weekend."

Something didn't feel right. "Um, okay. Well, I don't have much going on this week if you want to come over before the weekend."

"No, it's okay. I'll just call you later and let you know when I'm free this weekend."

It was odd. Like he was still holding a grudge. And for what? He was allowed to ask me a thousand questions about a little thing like losing my phone, but I couldn't question him about whether his 'business' was legit?

I grabbed my backpack from the rear of the car and closed the door. He didn't get out; instead, he powered down the passenger-side window.

I watched that, mouth slightly open. What was going on? He *always* got out of the car, walked me to the door, and gave me a kiss. Always.

"I'll call you later. Have a good night, Ava." Jonah said, leaning over the center console.

"Okay, see you later."

He didn't even wait for me to get to the door. I watched his taillights fading as he sped into the distance, a sick feeling growing in my gut.

Chapter Twenty-Two

Things went back to normal after that. This seemed to be a running theme with him. He'd get upset and start acting aloof, making me feel terrible like I did something wrong. But after a few days of making me wonder whether this was the end, he'd show up and act like nothing had happened.

Penny had always talked about the games guys played. I decided that if this was the worst of them, I was lucky. At least he didn't get me pregnant and then ignored me. *This* game, I could play.

By Christmas morning, everything was fine. He'd spent Christmas Eve with his family, and I'd been with mine since my Aunt Chrissy, Uncle Mark, and their daughter Mayra were over. We'd planned for him to come over to my house for Christmas dinner when all of my family got together. I was really looking forward to seeing him and giving him the special gift I'd gotten him.

I woke up to the smell of coffee and glanced at my phone. It was just after nine. I heard faint voices downstairs and got a little excited to open presents, so I grabbed my robe and rushed down.

"Merry Christmas!" I shouted, running into the living room, expecting to see my family gathered around the tree, sipping coffee and waiting for me. "You should've woken me up. I would've—"

I stopped when I realized that Jonah was sitting in the armchair my dad usually occupied. I could tell he was freshly showered because his hair was slightly wet, and he was wearing a bright red sweater.

Shocked, I just stood there for a moment, wondering if I was still dreaming. Then I said, "Oh. Hi, Jonah. Merry Christmas."

"Hi, Honey. Merry Christmas," my mom said, rising from the sofa and wrapping an arm around me. "Jonah surprised us."

"Oh. I didn't hear the doorbell ring," I said, still stunned. They were all wearing their pajamas, like me, but I suddenly felt completely self-conscious. My candy-cane pajamas and matching robe were cute but kind of babyish. And I hadn't even brushed my teeth. What if I had yesterday's mascara all down my face. Why was he here? It was only nine! "Jonah, I thought you were coming later."

"Yeah, I know. But I thought I'd come early to celebrate in the Christmas festivities with you and your family."

My mom said, "We are all just sitting around the tree opening some presents right now. Did you eat? Can I get you anything?"

"No, no. I'm fine, but thank you," he said, just as polite as ever.

I went over to give him a hug but stopped before I got there. "Morning. Sorry, I'm in my PJs, and I haven't—"

"It's not a big deal. You look gorgeous." Jonah said as he wrapped me in his arms.

I sat down on the floor in front of the tree and motioned Jonah to sit next to me.

"This one's for you, Jonah," I said as I passed him a present from my parents.

My mom cleared her throat. "Wait. Before presents... Ava, can you help me in the kitchen?"

"Sure." Her tone was worrisome. She sounded like she had a bone to pick, so I braced myself as I got up and followed my mom and aunt into the kitchen. When they turned to me, I knew they both weren't happy.

"Honey, you know we are happy that you've found someone special to spend time with, however, this house is a shared space, and we would appreciate it if you let us know when people are coming over," my mom said.

"I didn't know!" I blurted, incredulous that they would blame me for this. "I had no idea he'd come this early. I told him dinner would be at two. He wouldn't give me a definite time yesterday, but he said he was going to watch his cousins open gifts in the morning and be over in time for dinner."

Aunt Chrissy made a clicking sound with her tongue. "So, you didn't know he was on his way? He didn't text you or let you know?"

I pulled out my phone and double checked my messages from Jonah. "No, I didn't get any messages from him."

My mother said, "Well, he should be respectful of the fact that there are several people who live in his house who need to know when company is arriving."

Chrissy nodded. "Entertaining isn't easy. Your mom did a lot of work. This just surprised her, Honey. It's not too much to ask for you to be more considerate."

They were teaming up on me. Sighing, I said, "I understand, I'm sorry," and went back into the living room to talk with Jonah. While my father and uncle were in the middle of testing out some gadget they'd gotten, I whispered, "So, I thought you were staying home to watch your cousins open presents."

He shrugged. "I did. They woke up at six."

"Oh. I didn't realize they'd get up so early. You could've let me know you were on your way. We weren't expecting you to come over until later today."

His smile fell. "Is there a problem? I thought you'd be happy to see me and open presents together."

"Of course, I'm happy to see you. It's just that my mom wasn't prepared. She wanted to shower and whatnot. She said you should've let me know when you were on your way since other people live here.”

“I thought it’d be a nice surprise on Christmas morning to be here to celebrate the day with you and your family. If your mom thinks that’s a mistake, then I feel bad for her because I care about you, Ava, and I want to be here with you and your family during a special time of year.”

Wow. He was putting me before his family, sacrificing his time with the people he loved most for me? That was one of the sweetest things anyone had ever done for me. And he was right. My mom was always so by-the-book. She needed to learn to roll with the punches and understand not everyone did things the same way as our family. This gesture was one of love; how could anyone look down upon that?

“You’re so sweet, Jonah. I wish I could kiss you right now,” I whispered.

“Why can’t you?” He grinned mischievously.

I looked around at my family, who were busy looking at their presents. “We’re sitting right in the middle of my family.”

“Well, if you can’t kiss me, then I’ll kiss you.”

He leaned in and kissed my cheek. I blushed and looked around to see if anyone had noticed. Conversations around us did not seem to stop. No one noticed at all.

I grinned. “I want to give you your present in private. I was thinking after dinner.”

“I thought the same,” he said and winked, making me think it was something really personal and special. After all, *I* was special to him. He wouldn’t have dropped everything and come here so early if he wasn’t about to give me a fantastic gift. I couldn’t wait.

Despite the rocky start, it was the perfect Christmas. After we opened the family presents, we had breakfast together. Jonah chatted with everyone like he was one of the family. Then we went outside and played in the snow for a while with Mayra. After that, we had an amazing dinner of ham and all the trimmings. As I sat there with my belly full, holding Jonah's hand under the table, I decided I couldn't possibly be luckier.

After we helped clean the table, I decided it was time to exchange presents, so I nudged Jonah to follow me to my room. "Come on. Present time!"

"Your smile is the best present I could receive," Jonah said as we made our way upstairs.

I turned around to smile at him and realized he didn't have anything in his hands. I thought he must have put them in the living room earlier when he first came over. "Do you need to grab yours?"

"Nope. I'm good."

I looked for a bulge in the pocket of his sweater. Something small, then. Jewelry?

When we made it to my room, I grabbed the wrapped gift from my desktop and presented it to him proudly. "Here it is!"

He opened the card I'd made and smiled. "Wow. This is really nice." Then he took his time unwrapping the gift like he didn't want to ruin the paper. The second he opened it, he leaned over and kissed me.

"It has a message in it," I said, pointing it out.

He read it and looked at my photo. "Wow," he said again and kissed me.

"Do you like it then?" Ava asked when they broke apart.

"Ava, I absolutely love it. I especially love the picture of you. You look so sexy, and now I can look at you any time."

I beamed proudly. "I thought it'd be nice for me to be with you everywhere you went."

"Well, I'm always thinking about you, but now I can take you with me. I really like it."

My heart fluttered with happiness. My first gift for a boyfriend was a success.

After a moment of silence, I wondered why Jonah was stalling. Was this for dramatic effect? Finally, I said, "Did you leave your present at home or something?"

"No, no. I have it right here. I need you to close your eyes."

I smiled and closed my eyes. I could feel Jonah moving around me and bouncing on my toes, rubbing my hands together in excitement.

"Okay, open!"

Jonah stood facing me, a small piece of paper in his hands. "I want to read you a poem."

Okay, interesting. I smiled and listened as he recited the poem. It was short and had some flowery lines in it, like, "I always think of you and all the good times we've shared."

Honestly, it seemed a little vague and generic, like an anniversary card he'd copied from at the store. There was nothing specific to just *us*, no mention of things we'd done or talked about, no inside jokes that showed me he'd written it just for me. When he finished, I tried to keep a smile on my face. I hoped that he'd pull something else out of his pocket, but he never did.

Instead, he asked, "What do you think?"

"I think it's a very nice poem," I answered, even though I was disappointed. "Where did you find it?"

"I wrote it just for you."

"You wrote that?" I couldn't help but sound doubtful.

"Yes, I wrote it for you. See?" Jonah turned the paper around to show me, revealing his handwritten lines scratched on the crumpled paper. "I wanted you to know just how I feel about you. Just like when I gave you that necklace and asked you to be my girlfriend, I'm telling you now, I really care about you, Ava, and I like you a lot. Our time together has been so much fun, and I'm excited to keep dating you and see where this goes."

I smiled, feeling guilty for second-guessing him. After all, he *had* given me that necklace. This was special. "You're amazing, Jonah. This is the sweetest gift you could have made for me."

Still, I felt a little disappointed that I had put so much thought, effort, and money into his gift, and Jonah hadn't done the same. My fault, probably, because we hadn't talked about how much they were going to spend on each other's gifts. But he didn't even write the poem on a nice piece of paper or decorate it, especially for me. He could've at least done that. Instead, I almost got the feeling that he'd forgotten to get me anything, and had just copied that down from the internet, last-minute.

Stop it, Ava. This was nice. Besides, he's given you jewelry before. What were you expecting?

When he said, "You want to go for a drive?" I agreed, just because I was worried my face was about to betray the storm of feelings I had going on, and I didn't want him to be upset that I was upset with his gift.

We drove to the center of town, where there was a Christmas tree, and just walked around, snapping pictures of each other surrounded by the holiday décor. It worked wonders; after a little while, I'd totally forgotten about my earlier disappointment. But I guess I hadn't hidden it as well as I'd hoped because he said, "I'm sorry. You went out of your way to get me that custom wallet with the picture of you. You even handmade a card! I should've gotten you something better than a silly poem."

We stopped in front of the passenger door of Jonah's car. He kept looking down at the ground like he was waiting for me to say something.

"No! I loved the poem you wrote me!" I said, repeating what I'd already told him. "It was very thoughtful, and I thought our Christmas was perfect. I knew you needed a new wallet, and I thought you'd like to see a picture of me whenever you used it. It's not any more special than what you did for me."

He took my hands. "Ava, I love you."

"I love you too, Jonah."

Jonah wrapped his arms around me and kissed me. He slipped his hand under my jacket, and I could instantly feel the warmth of his hand on the small of my lower back. He kissed my neck, his breath warm on my skin.

"I love you, Ava," Jonah said as he nibbled on my ear. "I really do."

He kissed me even harder this time. He squeezed me close before dropping his hands to my waist. Then he moved his hands down the sides of my hips and back up the front of my thighs. I had my arms around Jonah as well, but I loosened my grip to let him touch my legs since it felt nice to have his warm hands everywhere. They continue up the front of my jeans, across my stomach and chest, and back to my face. He cupped my face in his hands and stared into my eyes, breathing out, "You are so fucking hot. I need you."

It was only when he grabbed my hand, placing it on the front of his pants, that I started to feel nervous. I felt the bulge through his jeans and was suddenly very aware of our surroundings. We were in a parking lot in the center of town. It was dark, and I didn't think there was anyone around, but it was public.

I brushed it lightly, hoping to pull away, but his hand pulled me right back. I knew that he'd want me to go further soon, but I hadn't expected it to be here like this. This time, he kept his hand over mine and moved it around a little. Did he want a hand job?

He was wearing jeans, and we were out in the open.

Slowly, I started rubbing the front of his jeans, hoping I was doing it right.

Jonah let out a quiet moan and kissed me deeper, and though I felt a little more confident that what I was doing felt good for him, I still didn't want to. Not here. He started moving to the side as he kissed me, fumbling with something behind me. I heard a creak and felt the car door open. Jonah broke away and opened the door to the back seat.

"I really need you," he said as he pushed down on my hips, maneuvering me onto the back seat. My backside hit the seat, and I backed up along the bench to let Jonah get in.

He closed the door and covered me with his body. Then he started kissing me again, tangling a hand in my hair.

I didn't know where his other hand was until I heard him unzip his pants. Then, he took my hand and guided it between us. I felt the warmth of his pubic hair, and then his dick was in my hand. It was so hot, so rigid, and I could feel the veins on it. I'd thought it would be smoother, but right at that moment, there was only one real thought in my head: *I'm in a parking lot holding Jonah's dick in my hand.*

I stopped kissing Jonah and looked around. The lot was dark and empty, but the buildings around us were all lit up, and there were people inside.

"Jonah, what are we doing?" I asked.

"It's okay. It's dark. No one can see us," he said quickly, leaning in to kiss me. He seemed to have no problem having his pants down around his knees.

"Okay, but what if someone comes out and sees us?"

"No one is going to see us. If anyone comes outside, they'll go to their car and drive home. It's fine."

I looked around a bit more. No one was around. And now Jonah was breathing in a way that made me think he was getting annoyed. So, I leaned into his kiss and moved my hand slowly up and down on his dick. I still felt hesitant, but Jonah was right; it was very dark in the backseat, and no one was around.

I took a breath and focused my attention on Jonah. This time, it felt different because I was touching him instead of him touching me. I was in control. I could decide what I did next and how far I wanted to go. And I did want Jonah to feel good, especially since he'd been so forthcoming about his feelings for me.

I started to feel more confident as my pace continued. His breathing got quicker, and he kissed me more passionately, urging me on, showing me how much he liked it.

But then, after a few moments, he brushed my hair back and grasped it all with one hand. Then he firmly pushed my head down until my cheek brushed his dick. I assumed he wanted me to put it in my mouth, but I had no idea what I was doing. A hand job was one thing, but a blow job was an unmarked territory, and Penny hadn't given me those tips she kept talking about.

I tried to lift my head up, but the weight of Jonah's hands kept me from moving. I didn't want to tell him I wasn't ready and make a scene, so I decided to just go for it.

I opened my mouth and took the tip in.

Almost instantly, I felt like I couldn't breathe. It didn't taste bad, but it felt too big like it wouldn't fit and didn't belong there. My lips were wrapped around Jonah's hard dick as he pulled my hair, making me move my head move up and down. He moaned as I struggled to breathe through my nose, my saliva coating my face.

I'd felt like I was in control before, but now Jonah was in control, and I just felt like he was using me. But I couldn't tell him to stop. I felt like I was going to choke. He suddenly pressed down so hard on my head that my face pressed up against his crotch, and his dick touched the back of my throat. Hot and dizzy, I nearly gagged as he held my head there.

I started to flail my hands as I tasted something sour and salty. *Let me up!* I wanted to scream, but I couldn't. My mouth was full, and I felt sick. I pulled my head up and drooled it all down my chin and onto Jonah's pants.

"Ah, c'mon, Ava. You couldn't have swallowed?" He shoved me off his lap and leaned forward to grab a napkin from the center console. "Fuck, now I'm going to have to get these cleaned."

"I'm sorry, I..." I heaved, trailing off. I was just trying not to pass out.

Jonah finished wiping off his pants as I wiped my face with the back of my hand. He took a deep breath and said, "It's okay. You were actually very good."

"I was?" I hadn't felt very good. In fact, I didn't want to do that ever again.

He smiled and gave me a quick kiss. He pulled up his pants and opened the car door. I was still a little stunned at how normal he was acting, considering it had felt so strange. I was glad he seemed happy, but I felt... wrong.

"Hey, let's get going. I have to get you home."

I crawled out of the backseat, and Jonah wrapped his arms around me and kissed me before helping me into the front seat. As we drove home, I wondered if that was what it would always be like to touch Jonah. Maybe it would get better. It had to, right? Penny always said it was no big deal. Once I knew what I was doing, it would be just fine.

And yet, something I couldn't quite put my finger on still bothered me. But I brushed it off, and we sang along to the holiday music on the ride home.

Chapter Twenty-Three

New Year's Eve came, and I was excited because Jonah had invited me to his house to watch movies with his family. Apparently, they had a tradition where his mother went overboard making appetizers, and they all pigged out until midnight. I hadn't gotten a chance to really talk to them during Thanksgiving, so I dressed nicely but comfortably in sweats and a zippered sweater, wanting to make a good impression.

My mom dropped me off at the Manzanos' house. "Have a good time, Dear."

I kissed her cheek. "Love you, Mom."

I rushed up the driveway and rang the doorbell. Mrs. Manzano answered. "Oh, hello, Ava! So nice to see you again."

She gave me a big hug as I walked into the foyer. It smelled like pizza and buffalo chicken wings, which made my mouth start to water. Then she peppered me with questions about how I've been enjoying the break and how school was going. I was proud that I stayed pretty calm, telling her about how midterms were right around the corner when we returned from winter break. I talked about how much fun Jonah and I had been having on our dates.

Mrs. Manzano seemed very sweet and really put me at ease. "It was really great to talk with you more today, Ava. You sound like such a sweet kid," she said, glancing up the stairs, which confused me. Weren't we going to spend the night watching movies together?

Just then, Jonah barreled down the stairs and grabbed my hand. "C'mon," he said, heading for the door.

"Wait. Where are we going? Aren't we...?"

He didn't stop until we were outside in his car. He unlocked the door, and I got in. When he jerked the car into reverse, he said, "Change of plans. I can't deal with them tonight."

"You can't?" No wonder he hadn't told them goodbye. I hadn't, either, and now I felt like a big jerk. Mrs. Manzano had been so sweet. "Were you having an argument?"

"You could say that," he muttered darkly, driving too fast out of his development.

"Where are we going?"

"To D-Phi. That okay? They're having a party," he said in a way that made me think that even if it wasn't okay, it wouldn't matter.

"Well..." I frowned. I hadn't told my parents about that. They wouldn't like the plans changing without them knowing. "I'm not really dressed for—"

"It's not a big deal. It's going to be pretty low-key since school isn't in session."

I hadn't been back to his fraternity since the last party. And that last time had been pretty terrible since he'd slapped me. I was just about to make up an excuse when he added, "Your friend is going to be there."

I blinked. Was he trying to be cute, bringing up that guy that had been flirting with me? "My friend?"

"Yeah. Penny."

That was news to me. I guess I deserved to be in the dark since I'd all but cut myself off from my friends over the past few weeks. "Really? What happened?"

He looked over at me. "You don't know?"

I shook my head. I hadn't had fun during our girl's night since they kept giving me a guilt trip for not spending enough time with them. After that, I'd pretty much given up. The way I saw it, if I tried to spend more time with them, Jonah would be upset. I couldn't win.

It irked me that he knew more about my best friend than I did. "Do you?"

He shrugged. "Not really. I just heard she and Kyle were hanging out again."

That was a surprise. So, she'd told him, and he was okay with being a father. I had a hard time believing that. Then again, I had a hard time seeing Penny as a mother. I'd missed big pieces of this story. My own fault.

Still, it made me feel better to know that Penny would be there. At least I could hang out with her.

Jonah wasn't kidding when he said that it would be low-key. The Icana campus was deserted for the winter break, and so was the house. When we walked inside, the living area that had once been packed with people was empty. There was no music shaking the walls. No dancing. No wild crowds, drinking beer, and creating havoc.

"There's a party here?" I asked, confused.

He shrugged. "C'mon. Let's go upstairs and watch a movie."

I thought about the last time I'd been in his room and actually shivered. "Wait. I thought we were having something to eat."

"Why? Are you hungry?"

I nodded. I was fairly certain Jonah had invited me for dinner, and now I was starving. "I didn't eat anything because I thought—"

"I'll make you some popcorn then."

Popcorn for dinner. Sure, why not? I didn't want to argue. I was so hungry, anything sounded good.

We went through a room I'd never been to. There was a giant wooden table in it that looked like something from a medieval banquet hall, and I could see all the Greek flags and paddles on the walls. He pushed open a swinging door that led to the room I'd been to before—the kitchen. As he did, I heard voices and saw a group of people gathered around a table there, holding cards. One of them was Penny.

"Hey!" they all shouted, mostly at Jonah, when we walked in. It was that one word and all the beer bottles scattered on the table that told me they were pretty drunk. One guy I didn't recognize with a D-Phi sweatshirt and a cinnamon beard said, "Jonah, my man. Join us."

Jonah grinned. "What are you playing?"

"Asshole."

At first, I thought the guy was insulting Jonah, but Jonah said, "Nah, just making popcorn," as he rummaged in a drawer and pulled out a bag. If that was the name of a game, I'd never heard of it. But Penny had and was clearly into it. She was holding her cards in one hand, a bottle of beer in the other, and talking with some of the guys nearest her. I waved at her, but I don't think she noticed me.

Was she drunk, too? Pregnant and drinking? That couldn't be good. I didn't care if she was purposely avoiding me because she was mad at me. I needed to talk to her.

As Jonah put the popcorn in the microwave, I went over to the table and leaned into Penny. "Hey. Show me where the bathroom is."

Annoyance flashed on her face, but she set her cards down, pushed away from the table, and stood. When she rocked back and forth, I knew she was definitely drunk. "Boys, don't start the next round without me. I'm President next time."

I looked at what she was wearing. She had a short skirt on, and her legs were bare, which wasn't a great idea considering how cold it was. But the old Penny had never cared about that stuff—all she cared about was boys and parties. It looked like she hadn't changed much.

As we went to the bathroom, I said, "Do you know how to play that game?"

She laughed. "Are you kidding? I've been totally cleaning the floor with them."

"Oh." I hesitated. "So, Kyle invited you over?"

"Yep." She took me down a long hall and stopped in front of a door, presenting it to me. "Here it is."

Even drunk, it was obvious she was holding a grudge. Before she could turn and leave, I grabbed her arm. "I'm glad everything's working out for you with him."

"It is," she said with a bit of defiance in her voice as she stared at my hand on her arm. "It's been amazing."

"That's really great," I said, wondering why it felt like we were strangers. This was the girl I'd met in kindergarten. How was it possible that so much had changed in only a few short months. Desperate to get back to that, I said, "I'm glad he's stepping up. So, when you graduate, are you going to—"

"I've got to get back," she said, her face falling. She shook herself free and turned abruptly.

"Wait," I said, horror flooding in as I realized what this meant. I followed her, and my voice was louder than I anticipated. "You told him, right?"

She didn't turn around, which gave me my answer.

"You *have* to tell him," I called after her. "It's not fair to him or you. And you shouldn't be—"

She turned then; her eyes narrowed to slits. "I *did* tell him. We had a long talk. And the more we talked about it, the more I realized it wasn't the best time for either of us. So, I made an appointment two weeks ago, and that's that."

"You..." She made it sound like a regular dentist's checkup. I'd assumed that if she did anything like that, she would want me, her best friend, with her. But if Kyle had stepped up, that was something. "Kyle went with you...?"

"No. He had exams."

Of course, he did the jerk. "I wish you'd have let me know. I would've—"

"What?" She spat out, hands on hips. "You would've come with me? After being MIA all this time? Then you'd go on and on about your perfect boyfriend while making the rest of us feel like shit?"

I blinked. Was that what she thought? Yes, it was true we'd drifted apart, but I'd thought it was more her doing than mine. Jonah had taken up a lot of my time, but she was the one who'd stopped calling me. "I don't. I—"

"Well, I've got news for you, sister," she said, slurring her words, and she poked me in the chest. "He's *not* all that perfect. Ask anyone who saw him at the party after finals."

I stared at her, confused. "What do you mean?"

Her bleary eyes went wide, making her look innocent. "Why don't you ask him?"

Then she turned and walked away, leaving me speechless.

My mind reeled back to finals the week before Christmas. It was practically already Christmas vacation at Wood Wil, with classroom parties and teachers only half-heartedly giving assignments. But Jonah had been busy because he'd been working on internship interviews and studying for finals. I'd had more time to myself, for sure, because he'd told me he had to stay on campus and study. He'd mentioned that it was hard to get things done because there were parties every night since some people finished their finals early.

But that didn't mean Jonah had gone to those parties. Penny

was lying, of course, out of jealousy. That had to be it. Because there was no way Jonah would hook up with other girls if that was what she was insinuating. He was always texting me, checking in on me. And he'd gotten so jealous when I was talking with that other boy during the last party. He'd never do something so low. That was Kyle.

Still, when I went into the bathroom and looked at my face in the mirror, I didn't recognize myself. I never thought I'd be the kind of person who would abandon my best friend in her hour of need, but I had.

And all those terrible things she thought about me now? Deep down, I knew I deserved all of it.

Chapter Twenty-Four

"Wow, your room looks different," I said as I walked into Jonah's room. He followed with the popcorn and drinks. "Cleaner."

"Yeah, I brought a lot of stuff I didn't need back home," Jonah said, setting the snacks down on the desk. "So, what do you want to watch?"

I gnawed on my lip. After the shock I'd gotten from Penny, I could've done with something light. I'd already thought 100 times about asking him if what Penny had said was true but decided it would only make him angry. And of course, it wasn't true. If I acted like I believed it, it would just destroy our trust in each other. But maybe there was a more subtle way of finding out?

"Uh, what do you have?" I asked, looking around his room for the tell-tale sign of cheating, an earring or lipstick smudge on his sheets. I sniffed the air, but it only smelled like his cologne.

"I've got a lot of horror." When I made a face, he winked. "Don't worry, we can cuddle so you don't get too scared."

"As long as we have time to watch the ball drop," I said, perching on the edge of his bed. A memory of the last time I was here came over me, and I shivered. "I didn't know we would be alone."

He grinned. "What, are you scared?"

"No. It just would have been nice to know what was going on."

"You do know what's going on. I just told you." His voice had an edge to it.

"Jonah, you told me we were going to have appetizers with your parents and watch movies. But then you whisked me off to your room in the frat." I sighed. No wonder my mother was so upset when he changed plans for Christmas.

He shrugged. "What's it matter? You came over to spend time with me, right? I don't know what you're getting so upset about. Aren't you happy we still get to hang out?" The edge got more pronounced.

I was worried it would boil over into full-blown anger, so I let it go. "You're absolutely right, Jonah. I came over because I want to spend time with you. Seeing your family and friends is nice, but it's you that I want. I'm glad we get to spend New Year's Eve together."

He sat down next to me and put a hand on my knee. "Thank you. I won't eat any of the popcorn since you're so hungry."

I laughed. We sat together against the headboard of his bed while Jonah flipped through the selection of movies. When we picked a movie, I cuddled up under Jonah's arm, the popcorn bowl between us. I took a handful and popped one in my mouth. "Hey. So, did you go to any of those after-final parties to blow off steam?"

He looked at me in the darkness as the beginning credits rolled. "Yeah. I guess. I think I made an appearance at one."

"Oh, cool," I said nonchalantly, already sensing his suspicion. "You have fun?"

"Nah," he said with a shrug. "Not without you."

I smiled, but it didn't feel like enough. He'd been at a party. Had he met someone? Was Penny telling the truth? My mind swam with questions, none of which I could ask him for fear of making him upset.

We were halfway into the movie when I sat up to put the popcorn bowl on the nightstand. When I leaned back over to settle into Jonah's arm again, he put his hand under my chin to bring my mouth up to his. He started kissing me softly and slowly. After a minute, I couldn't even hear the movie anymore. Everything was tuned out except for Jonah and his excellent kisses.

I'd been thinking about the blow job and wondering what I could do to make it better. I liked the way I made him lose control and wanted to do it again. Feeling emboldened, I ran my hands under his shirt and pushed it up over his head. I kissed down his neck and onto his collarbone.

"Ugh yeah, bite me," Jonah said.

I bit Jonah's neck just a little bit before nibbling on his ear lobe. I heard his breathing get heavier and went back to kissing him.

Jonah's kisses were more intense now. He started rubbing his hands on my thighs before moving them up my back and pulling my shirt off. He immediately went to unclip my bra, and it fell off in front of me. Jonah's hands cupped my breasts as he kissed my ear and neck all the way down to my nipple. He made sure to gently suck on both nipples before making his way back up my neck and to my mouth. It felt so good kissing Jonah with my bare chest pressed against his, but I kept hearing Penny's voice in the back of my head. *He's not so perfect...*

After a moment, I heard a zipper and felt Jonah's hand on the back of her head. I broke the kiss and looked down to see Jonah's jeans had been undone, and his dick was hanging out. I figured that was a sign he wanted a blow job, so I opened my mouth and went down on him.

"Yes, baby, that's it." Jonah said.

Jonah didn't put his hand on my head this time, which made me feel like the training wheels were off and that he enjoyed what I was doing. I felt confident as his dick got harder, but just as Jonah started moaning, he put his hands in my hair and pulled my head up. I wiped some saliva off my chin with the back of my hand. "Is everything—"

Instead of answering, Jonah planted his mouth right on my nipple again. This time, he bit harder, and I felt his tongue move faster as he pushed me back until I was lying flat on the bed. I felt him shimmy his legs until I heard his pants fall to the floor. Jonah's body was even warmer now, and his boner was pushing into my stomach.

Jonah's kisses were firm, like he knew exactly what he wanted, as he covered me with his body. As he lay on top of me, I felt like I couldn't move, and I could hardly breathe. I put my hands on his hips to try and lift him up a bit, but he was just too heavy. I tried to wiggle out from under him, but I was quickly losing air.

I turned my head to the side and broke away from Jonah's kiss. "I can't breathe."

"Yes, you can. You're talking to me right now." Jonah said with a smile and leaned back down to kiss me.

"Seriously, Jonah," I said, firmer.

"You're okay. Just get into it," he murmured, kissing my neck.

Annoyance flared in me. I needed a minute to calm down. I stiffened, and he must've felt it because he propped himself up on his elbows.

"Here. Is that better?"

It was. I let him kiss me this time and tried to kiss him back with the same passion. I tried to enjoy the feeling of his skin against mine.

But then Jonah reached for the hem of my sweatpants and started to pull them down. I let him slide them all the way off, but it was only when I was lying there in just my underwear that I started to get nervous. Were we going to do this tonight?

Jonah started to lean on my chest again, stealing my breath. I tried not to make a big deal out of it this time, but I was getting more and more afraid as his fingers flirted with the hem of my underwear. Jonah slipped his hand into my underwear and started caressing me.

I liked it, but not as much as I hoped I would. Honestly, it felt a little weird. I wondered if this is how it was supposed to be.

"Do you want me to use a condom?"

The question shocked me out of my thoughts. All the breath left my lungs, and my skin heated. "Uh. I like what we're doing. I don't think I'm ready for that right now," I admitted.

"Baby, we're so close. It's really not a big deal." Jonah said as he took his hand out of my underwear and started rubbing his dick on my abdomen. "Can't you feel how hard I am for you? I can make you feel so good."

It didn't really feel good. I wanted to go back to kissing and cuddling. "Jonah, I'm just not ready right now."

"We've been dating for a while now, and we love each other, it's only natural," he breathed out.

The weight of Jonah's body seemed to crush me. He wasn't listening to me. Not at all.

Fear spiked in me as I put my hands on his hips again and tried to wiggle out from under him again. "I—I do love you, but this is not the time. I just don't feel ready yet."

"Fuck," Jonah suddenly growled as he rolled off me and jumped to his feet. He didn't look at me, but his expression was one of disgust.

It made me feel like he hated me.

I sat up on the bed, looking for something to cover myself. "Jonah, I'm happy to keep making out and do other stuff, I just don't think I'm ready to go all the way."

"Do you know how many girls I can get to sleep with me, Ava? There's a college full of them!" Jonah paced by the bed. "When we met, you were at that party dressed like you were ready to jump into bed with the first guy that hit on you. I thought you wanted to sleep with me. Were you just there to tease me? Because that's all you've been doing since then."

I didn't know what to say. "I didn't mean to lead you on. I really like being with you. I do want to be physical with you, but this is my first time being with someone. Why can't we just take it slower?"

He let out a sour laugh. "Ava, we are going as slow as humanly possible. I have been patient with you and stopping whenever you want, but this is too much. You can't just get me all aroused and then not finish the job. I'm a guy. I need it, and if you're not going to give it to me, I'll get it somewhere else."

I blinked. "Is that what you've been doing?"

He exhaled and looked away, and at that moment, he didn't have to say a word. I knew it was true. "What do you expect? Who are you holding back for? I'm your boyfriend, Ava, you should be ready. I've paid for all our dates and bought you that expensive necklace. You've met my friends and family, and I've met yours. What else is there?"

I felt tears pushing at the corners of my eyes. But I didn't want to cry in front of him, so I stood up and picked my clothes up off the floor. "I want to go home."

"Don't be like that. It's not even midnight. We have plenty of time to have fun together," he said, his voice softer. He reached over and tucked a lock of hair behind my ear, and I thought I saw the sweet Jonah I'd fallen in love with. "You're my girlfriend and I love you. Let's get back into bed and mess around, okay?"

I hesitated, not sure if I believed he'd go slow. He'd been so worked up a minute ago that, frankly, it had scared me. "No. I think I want to go home."

Jonah stared at me. "Babe, I am not bringing you home. So, get back into bed, and let's enjoy the rest of the night."

I wrapped my arms around myself. This was a new side of him. He'd never outright refused to drive me home.

Finally, I said, "Fine, I'll call my mom and go wait downstairs."

I tried to move around him, but he grabbed my arm, his hand tightening like a vise.

Before I could react, Jonah's other hand flew up and slapped me across the face. The sting was immediate. My jaw tightened, and tears were instantly pulled from my eyes.

I reached up to touch it, but he grabbed my neck and pushed me face-first on the bed. "Wait, what are you—"

I couldn't say more because he pushed my nose and mouth into the blanket, making it impossible to breathe, much less speak.

"Now, you're going to stay on the bed and enjoy this," a voice that sounded nothing like Jonah said. I felt his hand at my hip, rough, pulling away my underwear and his legs between mine, prying them apart.

Then I felt the pressure of Jonah forcing himself into me. It was such a shock that I hardly registered the painful friction of him moving rapidly in and out of me.

Finally, Jonah stopped. The weight from the back of my neck was lifted, and Jonah flipped me over onto my back. He knelt over top of me and planted a strangely gentle kiss on my lips.

I couldn't move except to tremble. I squeezed my eyes closed as he said, "That's how good girlfriends are supposed to act."

He kissed me again before getting up and making his way out of the room.

I didn't know what to do, but the last thing I wanted was to upset Jonah again. I laid there for another minute before getting up and pulling my underwear and sweats back on.

"Look. Plenty of time. Told you!" Jonah pointed to the alarm clock as he came in. He acted as if nothing had happened.

"I'm going to the bathroom," I said cautiously as I slowly walked toward the door.

My mind was blank. I didn't know what to think or how to feel. I thought I wanted to cry, but no tears were coming. All I knew was that I wanted to be home in my bed. I sat there on the toilet, wishing my mom would come. I was bleeding, but I didn't have a tampon. I just stared at the red swirling in the bowl, feeling like I might throw up.

When I was done, I washed my hands and face and examined my jaw in the mirror. It didn't look nearly as bad as it felt. No one would even notice.

After I collected myself as best I could, I went back into Jonah's room to collect my things. When I got there, Jonah gave me a big hug. "I love you, Ava."

"Okay, love you too." I felt like I wanted to sprint away from him, but I knew I had nowhere to go.

Chapter Twenty-Five

The final bell rang, and everyone got up to escape school for the day. Listlessly, I stood. Every movement felt like a chore. I'd spent the rest of the weekend lying on the couch, binging on terrible reality TV. I'd eaten too many cheese curls and tried to ignore the outside world.

But I hadn't been able to. Jonah kept texting me, wanting to get together. I made excuse after excuse, but soon, I'd run out of them. At first, I thought I'd let Jonah apologize and explain his behavior on New Year's Eve. But the longer I thought about it, the more I realized there was no explanation for what he'd done. He was wrong. That was it.

"Ms. Parker, can you hold back a second?" Mr. Gunther said, pulling up a chair in front of his desk.

He pulled out a paper from a drawer and placed it on his desk for me to see. It had a big red D on the top. I cringed.

"Ava, you seem like a good kid. You've done well in this class so far, but your attitude over the last few weeks has really affected your grade. What's going on with you?"

"Nothing, Mr. Gunther. I just wasn't feeling well. Everything is fine. I'll study harder for the next test."

"The next test will be the midterm exam, so I hope so. I want you to pass the midterm and this class. You need to ask more questions in class if you are stuck and possibly get some extra tutoring."

My phone buzzed and I looked down at my lap to read the text. *Hey gorgeous. I'm in the senior lot, waiting for you.*

The words blurred in front of me. My stomach turned. I wanted to climb under a desk and never come out.

"Ava? Are you listening to me?"

I broke my gaze from the phone and looked up at my teacher. "Okay, Mr. Gunther, I get it. I will do better. Thank you." I pointed at my phone. "That's my mom. She's here. I have to go."

I stood up and power walked to the senior lot. Once again, Jonah was making the rules. The nerve of him! Before, I wasn't ready to see him, and now I wasn't sure if I ever would be.

As I opened the door to the lot, I saw Jonah leaning on the driver's side door with his arms crossed over his jacket. He still had his sunglasses on, and for a moment, I felt breathless, remembering what I'd seen in him. He was so cool that the other girls in the lot were looking at him, too. Now, though, it seemed like a disguise, hiding the real person underneath.

"Hey, baby," Jonah said as he stood up and leaned in for a kiss. I took a step back before he could reach me. "What are you doing here?"

"Here to see my beautiful girl," he said with a smirk. "Thought I'd drive you home."

I sighed. "Jonah, you can't just show up without telling me. I—"

"How else am I supposed to talk to you, Ava? You haven't answered any of my texts or calls."

I opened my mouth to speak, but he grabbed the door handle and opened it. "Get in the car, we can talk about this on the way."

For better or for worse, now was the time to talk. Jonah was here and ready to listen. As much as I didn't want to be in his presence, I had to do this right. Make a clean break. I climbed into the passenger seat and was quiet as Jonah turned the key in the ignition and started to drive away from the school.

"Ava, I came to talk to you because I love you, and it hurts me when I'm away from you. I haven't heard from you. You're my girl, and I want you to be happy. Being with you makes me happy.

Doesn't being with me make you happy?" Jonah said quietly as he stared out onto the road.

I sat there, silent, willing myself not to let his sweet words sway me. Not long ago, I'd have killed to be called "his girl." It was music to my ears. But now, it felt hollow. I most definitely hadn't been happy on New Year's Eve, and he hadn't cared. "I need you to take my feelings into account. It can't just be whatever you want to do."

Jonah pulled into our ice cream spot. The serving window was boarded up, and there were no cars in the parking lot.

"Babe, why do you think I came to the school instead of your house today? Because you're mine, and I can do whatever I want. You just have to accept it."

I blinked; not sure I was hearing him right. He couldn't mean that. I'd expected sweet words of apology, but not that. He didn't own me. I started to tell him that when he clamped a hand around my throat, making me catch my breath.

"You don't tell me what to do," he growled, squeezing.

I tried to take a breath but could only suck in air through my nostrils.

"I can make you happy, Ava. I have made you happy, haven't I?"

Jonah leaned forward and kissed me, with his hand still firmly around my throat. He slid his tongue into my parted mouth as I tried to suck in another breath.

"Now, kiss me back," he said as he moved his hand to cup my face.

I tried to take in a gulp of air, but Jonah's mouth was already on mine. I took a few shallow breaths through my nose to calm myself down, but he was in my face, holding me in place. Before I knew it, Jonah had his fingers wrapped in my hair.

He wrenched my head back, his hot breath on my throat. He pressed a few gentle kisses into my jaw before whispering in my ear, "I said, *kiss me back.*"

Dizzy and disbelieving, I kissed Jonah the way he wanted. I knew that if I didn't, he'd hit me again, or worse. I couldn't escape; he'd come get me. He wouldn't let me out of his sight until he got what he wanted.

Stupid, stupid! Why did you get in the car with him?

I let him rub his hands down my shoulders and arms. As he leaned over the center console, he unzipped my coat, his hands scrabbling underneath my sweater. It wasn't long after that I could hear the sound of his jeans unzipping.

I couldn't escape. He had me pinned against the door. I didn't know what was going to happen next. I just hoped it would be quick.

"Ava, you make me so hard. I need you so bad," Jonah said and sat back down in his seat.

I opened my eyes and saw Jonah's jeans down past his knees. His dick was standing straight up out of his boxers. Fear tangled my gut.

"I-It's still light out," I said to him, teeth chattering.

"The place is closed for the season. Don't worry about it." He reached for me, lacing his fingers through my hair. "Shh, baby, baby, be a good girl, like I know you can be."

Jonah's hand was firm as I leaned toward Jonah's lap. I opened my mouth and let him in. His legs were cold as my cheek brushed against them ever so slightly with each bob of my head.

Jonah grasped my hair tighter, groaning. I didn't care about making him feel good anymore. I thought about biting down or hurting him in some way to get this to stop. I let my lips fall back from my teeth and they grazed Jonah's dick. In response, he stiffened and pushed down harder on my head, forcing his dick deep down my throat. "Ahh, watch the teeth, babe!"

I was leaning awkwardly over the console, my nose pressed into Jonah's thigh. I saw myself, from up above, and how stupid and pathetic I looked. I'd spent so many nights and days thinking of this man, dreaming of being with him, and now, this was what we'd been reduced to. I'd gotten myself into this mess, and now, the only way out was through.

Trying to finish as fast as possible, I let my mouth go to town. He liked it, considering the way he loosened his grip on my hair and his breathing grew more ragged. Before I knew it, Jonah let out a loud moan. I tasted the warm, sour stuff in my mouth. I tried to swallow without gagging this time so Jonah wouldn't make a fuss. I gave a tug with my mouth to make sure no drops were left behind.

Then I picked my head up and slid slowly over to my seat, afraid of what might happen next. Jonah was leaning back in his seat, head tilted back, so I couldn't see his expression.

After a few seconds, he smiled and said, "You are so fucking good, Ava. I can't believe no one else snatched you up before me. I'm so lucky you're my girlfriend."

I let out the breath I'd been holding and relaxed a little as he started the car and searched for my hand, taking it from my lap. With me in the front seat of Jonah's car, his hand in mine, it probably looked like a normal trip home from school. But nothing was the same anymore. Absolutely nothing.

Jonah pulled into my driveway and looked at me, his face solid stone. "Call me before you go to sleep and let me know what you got into this evening."

"Okay, I will." I didn't look at him as I reached for the door.

I hoped he wouldn't touch me, but he reached for my arm

before I could get out, making me jump. "I want to be with you, Ava. I can satisfy you in so many ways. Just let me in."

His voice no longer sounded like music to me. It sounded eerie and scared me. My skin crawled where he'd touched me. I never wanted to get away from someone as much as I wanted to run away from him. "Okay. I know." I couldn't meet his eyes.

He pushed a lock of hair out of my face. "I love you. I'll talk to you later."

"I love you, too. Goodbye." My voice was wooden.

I couldn't get out of there fast enough. The first thing I did when I got inside was run to the bathroom and brush my teeth. Then I went to my bedroom and burrowed under the covers. But it wasn't enough to get me away from him. He would be calling me soon, and I would be expected to answer.

Chapter Twenty-Six

The next day, I sat there in the cafeteria, absently stirring the spoon around my pudding cup. I didn't feel like eating it, but I hadn't eaten anything all day, and I'd probably be sick if I didn't put something in my stomach. But lately, everything seemed tasteless. I stared down at the swirling chocolate, the sounds of laughter and clinking of trays nothing but faraway echoes.

"Wow, what are you doing here?" a voice said.

I looked up to see Sara and Penny walking toward me, and instantly felt a pang of longing for those old days, when it used to be the three of us, excitedly gossiping about school and boys. I thought I'd be excited to share the news of losing my virginity with my friends, but right then, I wasn't sure they were my friends anymore. Besides, I didn't want to think about Jonah. Whenever I did, I felt sick.

Penny put her tray on the table and looked me up and down. I thought for sure she would be able to tell I was no longer a virgin. Instead, she said, "What, no phone call from your college boy?"

My stomach turned at the mention of him. Yes, I'd spent most lunch periods in December on the phone with him, partly because he always called then, but also because I'd been sensing my friends' growing annoyance with me for constantly talking about him. But right now, a phone call from him was the last thing I wanted, which was why I'd sent a text to him, lying that I had some tests to make up.

"Not today," I said. "I thought I would catch up with you."

"Well, we're so happy to be graced with your presence," Penny said, and then she and Sara burst out laughing.

The sound made tears spring to my eyes. I thought that after I had sex, everything would make sense. I thought my life would be so much better. And now, I felt like crying.

I thought I would've enjoyed it more. For all Penny talked about it, somehow, she never told me that afterwards, I would bleed through a pair of underwear. I didn't know I would be sore and that it would still hurt to pee, three days later. And I didn't know that after we started, that would feel like *all* he wanted.

We could never go back to how it was before.

"Ava?" I heard Penny ask. "Are you not going to eat that?"

"I don't know. I'm not very hungry," I said without looking up.

"So did you guys have fun on New Year's?" Penny asked me.

I sighed. "I didn't think you wanted me to talk about that."

They both leaned in, and Penny said, "Ava...Is something wrong?"

I looked up, surprised to see genuine concern in her eyes. That was it. It was enough to open the floodgates.

"Actually, yes. I don't think I can do this anymore," I mumbled.

There was a long pause. I think they were both shocked by it. I was, too, but the second it was out, I was certain. I didn't want to be with Jonah anymore.

"Wait..." Penny said, her voice a whisper. "Is this because of what I said that night?"

I shook my head, confused at first. Then I realized she meant the whole thing about him cheating on me. At first, I'd dismissed it, but now that I thought about it, it was most likely true. I didn't know Jonah anymore. "It's more than that. I just... can't explain it. But you're right. You were right about everything. And I think I'm done. In fact, I *know* I am. I don't want to see him again."

Penny said, "Wow. Okay. So, you don't want to be with Jonah anymore," almost as if she had to force it through her head. "You know, good. I don't think he's good enough for you, anyway."

"But if I end it, he won't leave me alone." I said, trying not to sob all over the cafeteria table as I held up my phone. There were a bunch of texts from him. "I don't know how I'm going to break it to him."

"Oh, honey, I'll take care of that." Penny grabbed my phone from the side pocket of my bag.

A few moments later, she handed my phone back. "He won't be bothering you anymore," Penny said with a satisfied smile.

I looked at my phone. "How do you know?"

"Because I blocked him."

My eyes went wide, and panic seized me. "What?"

"Penny! You can't break up with someone over text. Ava should tell him in person that she's no longer interested in him," Sara said.

The thought of seeing Jonah, especially now that I had his number blocked, made nausea swirl in my gut. I was afraid of seeing him in person. If I saw him, he might threaten to hurt me and force me to change my mind. Once again, I was in his room, his hand holding me down, rendering me completely powerless. I pushed the pudding cup away. "I can't see him anymore."

"No. If she doesn't want to see him anymore, she doesn't have to. Problem solved," Penny said, surely.

I wasn't naïve enough to think that was the end of my problem. The moment Jonah realized I'd blocked him, there would be hell to pay. He might even come to the school, make a scene. He loved making scenes, showing up when I least expected it. I wasn't safe, even in my own classroom.

I scrambled to unblock it, my hands shaking. "I don't know."

When I looked up, Penny was staring at me. "Ava... are you okay?"

No, I wasn't. Now more than ever, I knew that Jonah played by his own rules and that there was no telling what he might do. I'd never been so scared.

But I couldn't tell her that. Penny always knew what to do with men to make them happy. She'd never been in a situation like this. She'd navigated the whole thing with Kyle and emerged unbroken on the other side. I didn't think I would be that lucky.

I muttered, "It's fine. I'll deal with it."

The bell rang, and I got up to leave. A short while later, Penny fell into step beside me. "Are you sure you're okay? You look terrible."

"Thanks," I mumbled. She'd been so quick to dismiss me on New Year's, but now she wanted to talk to me? That didn't make sense. Unless she was trying to hide something from me. "How is everything with you and Kyle?"

"Fine," she said in a small voice. "I mean... I don't know. Sometimes I think it's not going to work out, but whatever. It's fine."

"Yeah?"

"Yeah. I mean, he was nice and everything, giving me the money to go to the clinic. But then he didn't even want to go with me. He made all these excuses, and..." She let out a nervous laugh. "Making me go through that alone? Not cool."

I stopped walking and stared at her. "Wait. Penny... *did* you go to the clinic?"

She gnawed on her lip, looked up and down the hall, and then shook her head.

"Why not?"

She sighed. "Kyle wouldn't talk to me unless I said I'd go. When I said I would do it, he was so sweet. Said he'd pay and everything. And then he was so nice to me after... after I said I went. You know, checking in to see if I was okay."

I gaped at her. "But you *didn't* go?"

She shook her head slowly, tears in her eyes. "I can't. I couldn't. But I can't do this alone."

Maybe it was that she looked just as worried as I felt, but all the fear suddenly left me, and I was left with another emotion: Anger. I took her arm. "You're not alone. But you don't need Kyle. You have me. I'll help you."

"You've been so busy with Jonah. I thought you didn't care anymore."

"No, Penny. You're my best friend. It's you and me, forever, right?" I said, feeling stronger now as I held up my pinky to hers. We hadn't done that since we were in grade school, but she knew exactly what to do. She hooked her pinky with mine and shook it, a smile spreading across her face. "And I think it's time we find a way to kick these boys to the curb."

She nodded with the old Penny confidence I hadn't seen in her recently. "I think you're right."

"You want to come over to my place after school? I think we need to catch up."

She smiled. "Yeah. Sounds good."

I put an arm around her, and for the first time, I felt a glimmer of hope. Maybe we couldn't go back, but moving forward in the right direction could be just as good.

Chapter Twenty-Seven

After talking to Penny, I blocked Jonah's number for good. We went to my house and made cookies and gossiped together, just like in the old days. After that, I realized that those days weren't over. I'd just been passing over them for something I believed was better.

It was only while I was with her that I was finally able to take a step back and realize how wrong I'd been. Jonah was an abuser and had been gaslighting me all along. He didn't love me. He wanted someone to control, and I'd been so new to having a boyfriend that I'd let him.

I wasn't naïve enough to think that that was the end, though. Jonah had a temper, that much was sure. But Penny said that after a few days, he'd get the hint. She said most guys didn't have to balls to just show up at their ex's house and make a scene. I wasn't so sure about that, though. Not after what I'd been through.

But with Jonah out of my life, things started to get better. I was able to concentrate on my work again, and midterms went well. I was also able to put in a few applications to colleges. All of the schools were farther away—Pittsburgh, Philadelphia, even New York City. My dad was happy to hear that I'm excited to leave my hometown behind and see new places.

Part of that was true, but I also had an irrational fear that I'd run into Jonah if I stayed around Seagreen. Everywhere I went, I thought I saw his face.

After a few weeks had gone by, though, I eventually started to believe Penny. It was over. I was free.

One Friday night, Penny invited us over to her house to hang out. As we piled into her new car, the two girls blabbed about the newest drama at school. Truthfully, I'd lost interest and couldn't wait for graduation, when I could finally get away to college. My eyes started to drift toward the window as I daydreamed about walking across the stage at graduation, moving forward into a new life.

Penny's mom stopped the car at a red light, and I glanced out the window. The car behind us looked a lot like Jonah's. I blinked. Was I imagining things? I moved forward in my seat, trying to see who was in the car, but all I could see was the outline of a person behind the wheel. It was the right size and shape. It *could* have been Jonah.

"What are you looking at?" Penny asked me.

"I think that's Jonah's car," I said, pointing behind me.

"It can't be," Penny said, looking out her window. The light turned green, and the car made a left turn. I let out the breath I'd been holding.

"A lot of people drive those types of cars. Don't worry about it. Jonah knows you guys are done," Penny said to me.

"Yeah, Ava, you haven't spoken to him in a few weeks, right? He knows it's over," Sara added. I sat back, feeling a little better.

"Speaking of Jonah, we have a good idea of how you can get over him," Penny said.

"We just thought you've been pretty hung up on him and it might be good to explore your options," Sara said. Apparently, they'd discussed this without me.

I looked between them. "What options? Like a hobby?"

"Sure, like a hobby," said Sara with a wink.

"No, not like a hobby. Like a new man!" Penny said.

I groaned. Why would they think that was something I would want? I'd only broken up with Jonah a few weeks ago. I didn't need to worry about some new guy already.

"Don't worry. We've found one for you. He goes to East Central," Penny said.

"He's really cute. Penny, show her a picture," Sara said.

Penny whipped out her phone and showed her the photo. "His name is Dayton," she said.

The picture was of a tall, lanky kid with a short, dark beard and dark eyes. I had to admit he was cute. A different sort of cute than Jonah, but still cute. And things had gotten better since I'd ended it with Jonah. Things with the girls were back to normal, and we were hanging out almost every weekend. I no longer thought about him 24/7; in fact, I was able to concentrate on my schoolwork and other hobbies. I'd even started doing double shifts at the Seagreen Valley Animal Shelter on Saturdays, getting in my cuddles with the animals. I felt happy and proud that I'd come so far in such a short time, especially since not very long ago, my entire existence had been entwined with Jonah's.

Still, the thought of being alone with another guy and getting into the same mess as I'd gotten into with Jonah hung over me. I knew every guy wasn't like him, but that didn't mean I wanted to take that chance.

"No. I'm not interested," I said.

"C'mon, Ava. He really wants to meet you!" Penny said.

I gaped at her. "He knows about me? I thought you just wanted me to think about talking to him."

"Well, we figured you'd say no, so we took it upon ourselves to arrange the date for you," Sara said.

"What?"

"He's nice and handsome, and there is no better way for you to get over Jonah," Sara said with a shrug.

"Jonah isn't worth your time. It was fun, but now it's over. This new guy will be even more fun, I promise," Penny said with a wink.

"Ugh, Penny, no, I don't want to go out with some sleazeball."

"Oh, please. Do you think I would do that to you? Dayton is a nice guy, very respectable, and he's our age. He wants to take you out. Just go out with him for a few hours, and you'll be home and back in bed by ten. Scout's honor." Penny held her hand to her heart when she said this last part.

I rolled my eyes. "When is this date?"

"Tomorrow," they said in unison.

My jaw dropped.

"I know it's short notice, but that's why we invited you over. We'll help you pick out something to wear," Sara said.

"So, you invited me over to give me a makeover to go out with a guy I never met and have no interest in going out with?" I mumbled.

"Yep, that's exactly right, and it's going to be a blast!" Penny said with a grin.

I sat back in my seat while Penny and Sara talked about what nail polish color would look best on me. What if this guy turned out to be like Jonah? I'd have to be careful, and going out alone with him wasn't being careful. Did I want to take that risk?

No, at that moment, I just wanted to crawl into bed and wake up when the date and the uncertainty was over.

"Actually... no," I said, summoning the courage. "I don't want to go. Seriously. I don't really want to see anyone right now."

Penny said, "Oh, come on. He's—"

"*No*," I said again. "Really. And that's final."

The two didn't speak, but I could sense them exchanging looks. The second I said it, I wondered if it was the right thing to do. I should've wanted to move on from Jonah. But I felt stuck, frozen from fear.

"Maybe we could do, like, a group thing?" Penny suggested, reading my mind.

I looked up and nodded. They really weren't going to let this go. And I wouldn't mind hanging out with the girls some more. Yes, that would be the best way to ease into seeing other guys. "I guess I'd be okay with that."

Penny smiled. "Then let's do it."

Chapter Twenty-Eight

Damn it, I thought as I wiped away a black smudge from the corner of my eye. I was so nervous, I couldn't keep my hand straight enough to apply my eyeliner. *Why did I agree to this again?*

All day Saturday, I'd gone back and forth, alternating between thinking going out on this group date was a great idea, to wanting to hide under my bed for the night. Now, it was almost 8 pm, and Penny was on her way to pick me up. Her mom let her borrow the car for the night so we could stay as long as we wanted. The worst part about not having my own car was that I wouldn't be able to leave if I wanted to. I was Penny's captive, cursed to stay as long as Penny was having a good time.

And Penny was doing well. She'd broken up with Kyle and told her parents about the baby, who were supportive. They were both retired, so they'd agreed that they would babysit Penny's child while she went to Icana next year. She wasn't showing yet, and so everything was back to nearly normal for her.

I wish I could've said the same for me. I was still seeing Jonah everywhere I went. Even when I just closed my eyes, he was there, in my nightmares. I wasn't sure I'd be able to act normally around another guy, ever again.

As I strapped on my high-heeled boots, I took a deep breath, preparing myself to be charming. I'd have to laugh at Dayton's jokes, flirt with him, and put on a front. The thought exhausted me.

A few minutes later, Penny messaged me that she was outside. Showtime.

"You look great!" Penny and Sara exclaimed in unison when I reached the car. I knew they were just trying to butter me up, so I didn't turn around and escape back into the house. To be honest, as I slid into the back seat, I looked back at the house, wishing I could be back in my bed, asleep.

But the moment I closed the car door, Penny sped off for the arcade, and all opportunities to escape evaporated. I took a deep breath, willing my heart to slow down.

When we got to the arcade, the guys we were meeting were already there. Penny waved at them and rushed to meet them through a dark tunnel of flashing lights from the games. They were all playing air hockey. "Dayton. This is Ava!" Penny made a point of saying after he scored a goal.

He smiled at me and shook my hand. "Ava. I'm glad you made it."

"Hi," I said. There might have been a spark, but I was already feeling too awkward and nervous to feel it.

We all watched and chatted as the guys finished up their game. Then we bounced around from game to game, laughing and joking around. Dayton was sweet, always asking me to play with him and swiping his card when I ran out of tokens. We talked a little, and I learned he was a couple of months younger than me, but that was okay. Anything that made him less like Jonah, I figured, was a good thing. The smile I'd forced at the beginning of the night soon came naturally, and after a while, I forgot all about Jonah.

As the night died down, we split up to spend the last of our tokens on our favorite games. Dayton asked me if I wanted to play one last game of Skee-Ball.

I laughed as Dayton missed every ball. I wasn't very skilled at the game, but at least I could sink a couple of balls.

I was still laughing when Dayton turned and slipped his hands over my hips. Instantly, I stiffened and sucked in a breath, remembering how Jonah had touched me, as Dayton said, "I had a great time tonight. You're a lot of fun, Ava. Can I kiss you?"

A familiar chill went down my spine. The first instinct was to pull away. I gently pushed his hands off my waist. "Dayton, you seem like a nice guy, and I did have fun tonight, but I have to be honest. I just got out of a relationship and really don't think I am ready."

He took a step back. "No, it's okay. I'm glad you were honest with me. You'll be okay, just give it some time. On the bright side, you have friends who really care about you."

He pointed over to where Penny and Sara were watching with interest. I smiled. "They're insane, but I'm happy they're on my side."

Chapter Twenty-Nine

A week later, I got a surprising text from Dayton: *Want to meet for coffee? Just friends. J*

I looked at it and smiled. He was persistent. And so was Jonah. My smile dissolved, and I typed in: *Sorry, I'm not a big coffee drinker.*

I started to put my phone away when I received another text from him: *Actually, I have something I need to tell you.*

That piqued my interest. I'd only met him once. How was it possible he had something he needed to tell me? *What?*

I waited anxiously for his next words, but they were a letdown: *I'd feel better telling you in person.*

So, I arranged to see him in a shop near my house in twenty minutes. Then I quickly got ready and ran all the way there. When I walked in, Dayton was sitting at a small table on the side wall, nursing a to-go cup. He waved when he saw me.

"Hey, what're you drinking?" I asked, sliding into the seat across from him.

"Hazelnut mocha. Do you want anything? I can go grab it for you."

That was nice. For a second, I wondered what would have happened if Penny had introduced me to Dayton before bringing me to that college party a few months ago.

"No, that's okay."

I thought there would be a bit of awkward conversation, but luckily, he just went right into it.

"So, listen. A guy messaged me on Instagram. I think he was your boyfriend, or ex-boyfriend? He said some pretty bad things..." His face was turning red, and he clearly seemed uncomfortable, and he dug in his pocket. "Here, I'll show you."

Dayton showed me his phone. There was a photo of all of us from the night at the arcade, and Dayton had his arm around me. He clicked on his messages, and I saw one from *jmazz*. It said, *Back off, you piece of shit. You touch her again, I'll find you.*

I gasped. It had been a month since I'd blocked Jonah's number. And now, he was threatening people I'd been hanging out with? Nothing had even happened. So much for Jonah, moving on. "I am so sorry. We are not together anymore."

He shrugged. "I don't know this guy, so I'm not really worried about myself. I am concerned for you, though. This guy seems pretty possessive."

"It's okay. I have him blocked and I haven't seen him in a month," I said.

"I don't know, he's clearly thinking about you," he said, pointing at the phone. "I think you should tell someone. This guy is clearly unstable if he's getting up in arms about an innocent picture."

As much as I appreciated Dayton looking out for me, I wasn't too worried. It was easy to get wrapped up in the spur of the moment and type out a thoughtless comment. I'd been tempted to before, whenever I saw something I didn't like on social media. But I hadn't seen Jonah in a month. He had kept his distance. He hadn't shown up at my school or tried to contact me through friends.

I sat with him and chatted until he finished his coffee, and we walked out of the shop together. "I really appreciate you trying to warn me," I said to him as we stepped out under the overhang and onto the curb.

"No problem. I have sisters, you know. If they were in this situation, I'd tell them to run as far away from the guy as possible," he said with a grin as we waited for a car to pass.

As soon as we reached the parking lot, someone in a black hoodie came charging toward us. "I warned you!" It all happened so fast.

I stood in shock as Jonah plowed right into Dayton, tackling him. The two bodies skidded to the cement, and Jonah began pummeling him with both fists. I stood there in horror, hardly able to believe this was happening. Jonah, his hair wild and his face unshaven, looked like a madman.

"Stop!" I shouted, trying to grab him off Dayton. But he was wild, his fists lethal, and I knew what he could do to me with those hands. "Get off him, Jonah! There's nothing going on. Leave him alone."

But he just kept laying into poor Dayton, almost as if he didn't hear me. His punches were a blur, and as he continued to hit his victim, I saw blood splattering.

I screamed for him to stop until finally, Jonah gave him one last punch to the nose and then got up, breathing hard. Dayton lay on the ground, moaning in pain. He was still conscious, but I could see blood dribbling from his nose and red welts on his face.

"You want to defend this guy?" Jonah said as he swiftly kicked Dayton in the ribs. "You need to learn a thing or two about loyalty."

Jonah turned to look at me, and then suddenly charged me. He hit me in the waist, making me topple over his shoulder, then grabbed me and hoisted me up. I kicked and screamed, trying to get free as he carried me away. Then I heard the door open, and he shoved me into the passenger seat of his car, locking the door as he slammed it shut.

Before I could protest, Jonah climbed into the driver's seat and whipped out of his parking spot and onto the street.

He drove fast out of town, and I kept my fists clenched in my lap; my mind was swimming with fear. What could I say to him to get him to stop and let me go home? As the car barreled past houses in a blur, I saw a familiar street and finally realized where we were headed. We were a few streets from Jonah's house.

I took a deep breath. He wouldn't hurt me if he brought me home to his family.

But as we turned down Jonah's street, my heart sank. There were no cars in the driveway. There was probably no one there. It was a Saturday afternoon, after all. By the time we pulled into the driveway, all the relief I'd felt had vanished.

You can't go into that house! A voice screamed inside me. But it didn't look like I would have a choice.

He threw the car into park, got out, and opened my door. "Get out."

I stared straight ahead. "Don't do—"

Jonah grabbed my arm. "I said, *get out.*" He yanked my arm up, and my body followed. My feet thudded to the ground.

As Jonah pulled me toward the house, his jacket rode up on his hip, and I saw what looked like a hunting knife in a holster. Fear spiked in me. It felt like I wasn't in my own body, or I was in a dream. My feet were moving forward, even though I was willing them to stop and run in the opposite direction. I could barely feel how hard Jonah was gripping my arm. All I could do was focus on the front door. I had no idea what lay beyond it.

If I went in, would I ever come out?

I stood frozen on the front stoop as Jonah fumbled with the keys. A moment later, he opened the door, and I stumbled through the doorway with a slight push from Jonah telling me to get inside. I looked around the living room, surveying the scene while Jonah turned and locked the door behind us. The room looked the same as the last time I was over. Nothing new or surprising, unlike Jonah's behavior last time I was here.

We stood quietly for a few moments. The silence disturbed me. I couldn't read Jonah. The images of Dayton's bloody face were still racing through my mind, along with a thousand other thoughts, as the silence tore on. What was Jonah planning? Would he use that knife on me?

Jonah snapped me out of my head when he started rambling about how I'd betrayed him. He spoke so fast; I could barely keep up with his train of thought.

"Going out with another guy," "Ignoring my calls," "Making me feel like I was crazy for loving you," "You never cared about me."

He droned on and on as I tried to keep up. But Dayton was right. Jonah *was* unstable. And there was no telling what he would do to me, in this frame of mind. I had to try to calm him down.

"You made me look like a fool!" Jonah yelled in my face. He pulled the knife out of its holster and pointed it at me. "Did you think I wouldn't find out?"

I shrank back as Jonah and the knife got closer. He seemed to be wanting for an answer, so I swallowed and spoke.

"Nothing happened with Dayton," I said calmly, placating him as my mind went into overdrive. *Flatter him. Tell him what he wants to hear.* "You are the best boyfriend I've ever had. I could never make you look like a fool because you are the whole package. I made such a mistake, ignoring you for the last few weeks. I miss you every day, I just didn't think you'd take me back. I don't deserve you."

Jonah's face softened a bit, so I went on.

"I mean it. No one could replace you. No one knows me better than you. No one could love me better than you. Could you ever forgive me?"

I could see the wheels in Jonah's head turning as he processed this information.

"Why say this now? You've been ignoring me for weeks without seeming to care about me at all," Jonah snapped.

"I was embarrassed. You are so perfect, Jonah. You're handsome and smart and charming. You make me laugh and do so much for me. Any girl could have you, and there are so many girls who are more deserving of you. I was scared you'd break up with me the longer we were together. I was scared you'd find someone better, and I would be broken. I have regretted losing you. You showing up for me today just proves that you've missed me, too. So, please, Jonah, let's not waste any more time and just be together."

Jonah stared into my eyes as if he could pull the truth right out of me. I stared back, afraid to say more. Afraid to even breathe. *If I get out of this, I'm not making the same mistake twice. I'm going to the police.*

"Prove it," he finally said. His hand slowly lowered until the knife was down by his side.

"What?"

"Show me how much you missed me and what you're willing to do to get me back." Jonah's face looked smug.

I hadn't thought that far ahead. I honestly didn't think he'd believe me. Now that he had asked me to prove it, I knew I had to be very convincing. I took a step closer, cupped Jonah's face, and softly kissed his lips. After a moment, I could feel some of the tension slip away. Still aware of the knife in his hands, I deepened the kiss and closed the gap between our bodies.

I moved my hands down Jonah's chest and waist. I slid my hands underneath his shirt and up his back. I slipped my tongue into Jonah's mouth and kissed him like it was the last time I'd ever see him again. I bit Jonah's bottom lip and then pulled away, which I knew he liked, giving Jonah a devilish grin. I grabbed his free hand and walked him over to the couch.

Jonah smirked as I lowered us both onto the couch. I continued to look playfully into his eyes while I unbuckled his jeans. Once I loosened them, I put my mouth back on Jonah's. I traced my hands down his arms until I got to his hands, where I slowly pulled the knife out of Jonah's hand and placed it behind him on the couch.

My heart skipped as I waited to see if he would care or even notice. A moment passed, and no complaints.

I reached down and guided Jonah's dick out of his boxers. I gently stroked him all the while, wondering if I would be able to get out of the house once this was all over. I wondered if I would ever make it back home.

Jonah was kissing me back and even started running his hands through my hair. Jonah's dick grew harder as he let out a soft moan and I tightened his grip on my scalp. Jonah was clenching my hair so hard; my head pulled back and exposed my neck. I felt his hot breath on my skin as he kissed my neck all the way up to my ear. He breathed heavily for a second before saying, "You're such a bad girl. You're just looking to get punished, aren't you?"

I could feel the tears starting to well up in my eyes. Jonah was sick if he thought I enjoyed this; enjoyed submitting to him out of fear. I didn't know how he planned on punishing me, but I knew I'd have to go along with it.

Jonah started kissing me more aggressively, until there was a faraway sound. At first, I thought I was imagining it, but then it came again.

A knock at the door. My heart leapt. It could've been anyone, but my hope was that Dayton had somehow found out where Jonah lived and was here to help. Probably a fool's hope, but I held my breath, waiting to see what Jonah would do.

"Let me see who that is really quick," Jonah said as he got up off the couch. Taking deep breaths, I sat perfectly still, trying to hear what was being said, but I was too far away to make out any words.

"Ava, can you come here for a second?"

I cautiously got up off the couch and walked toward the front door. As I peered around the corner, I heard Jonah continue, "Can you tell these nice officers that everything's fine?"

The police! I stopped behind Jonah and saw not one, but two men, each about six feet tall. They were in their navy-blue officer uniforms with their vests and utility belts. Both of them could end this right now if I wanted them to. They were watching me, waiting for an answer.

Jonah was watching me, too. I could see a desperation in his eyes, but also a coldness that scared me to death. He'd be angry when we were alone again. So angry.

I opened my mouth to say what he wanted me to say, but I couldn't get any words out. Instead, I covered my face with my hands and burst into tears.

The officers took this as an answer. I stood there, frozen in place, tears streaming down my cheeks and sucking in shallow breaths. When the tears started to slow down, I saw Jonah, handcuffed, crawling into the back seat of the police car. Once he was seated, the officer closed the door, and Jonah hung his head, not looking at me.

I stood there in the doorway, my heart beating slower and slower until the world around me grew quiet. I knew this wouldn't be the end, but at least for now, I was safe.

Chapter Thirty

I sat in the police station, cradling a cup of lukewarm hot chocolate in my hands and shaking. Every so often, the receptionist would look over at me and ask how I was doing.

But I wasn't sure. I felt numb. Like everything that happened was just a nightmare, I couldn't believe that I was here, that Jonah had attacked and kidnapped me, that I'd somehow survived a situation that could've wound up very different. It felt like I was just waiting for the alarm to go off so that I would wake up.

"Honey," she said sweetly to me. "You're going to have to go in and give a statement to Detective Braun in a bit. All right?"

I looked around, still afraid that if I said the wrong thing, Jonah would come after me. For the past month, I'd been doing so well. But now, I wondered if I would ever move on from him. Could I? Or would he always be there, haunting me, making me afraid of my own shadow? "Jonah—"

"He's in a cell, in the back. You don't have to worry. You won't see him," she assured me.

I gnawed on my lip. I'd told myself I wouldn't see him again after I had blocked him, and yet, he'd found me.

"Ava!" a voice shouted from the door.

I looked over and let out a breath of relief when I saw Penny, followed by my parents. They all wrapped me in a hug, and Penny said, "I was so worried about you! When Jonah attacked you, Dayton called me, and I called your parents, who called the police."

I started to sob. I was so glad that there were good people in the world who were willing to help, including Dayton, who barely knew me. It gave me a brief glimmer of hope as my mother brushed the hair from my face. "You're okay. You're safe now."

My father said, "I never expected... we wish we'd known..." his face full of regret.

"It's okay, Dad," I assured him, feeling better now that I was here with people who loved me. "It's not your fault."

My parents went up to the counter to talk to the police, and Penny sat next to me and hugged me again. "It's not your fault, either," she whispered to me. "Don't ever blame yourself. I was the one who was so hot on going to the fraternity. What a mistake that turned out to be, huh?"

I hugged her tighter. "Why don't we put the blame where it belongs? On him."

She nodded. "Yeah. On him. Exactly."

I relaxed against her, my best friend, and it occurred to me that though I'd once thought losing Jonah would be the end of the world, it now felt strangely good. I hadn't realized it before, when I was so hungry and eager to get ahead in life, but I'd already had everything I needed. Friends, family. Maybe the one good thing about meeting Jonah was that now, I realized it, and wouldn't ever take them for granted again.

I didn't always have to move forward. Staying in one place was a choice, too, and right now, I was just fine with that. "But we're okay. Right?"

She pulled away, tears in her eyes, and smiled. "Right. Whatever happens, from now on, we've got each other. We'll get through this together. You and me, forever!"

She held out her pinky to me, and I hooked it with mine.

Epilogue

June 15th is our graduation day.

Penny thought she'd be able to make it there, but baby Olivia had other plans.

After the ceremony on the Wood Wil football field, I drove Sara to the Seagreen Memorial Hospital to surprise Penny and meet her daughter for the first time. Yes, I finally got my license, and my parents gave me my own car for graduation. Just a little beater, but enough to get me from point A to point B. I'm planning on working at the ice cream shop all summer to make up money before college, so I need a set of wheels to get me there. And then... college in New Jersey. I've decided to study business, and I'm excited about the thought of going somewhere I've never been, having true independence, and moving past the borders of Seagreen.

We walk into the hospital wearing our graduation gowns and caps, carrying flowers and balloons, and people congratulate us as we go up to the maternity ward.

Penny looks amazing, as usual. She's sitting up in bed, surrounded by her parents. Her eyes light up when she sees us.

"Congratulations!" we cry as we present her with her diploma.

"Wow, guys, how was it?" she asks, opening the folder and looking at her diploma.

"It was fine, but we missed you," Sara says, putting her graduation cap on Penny's head.

Next to her is the bassinet with baby Olivia, sound asleep. We both go close and gaze at the perfect baby girl. "Wow," I say. "She's beautiful."

Penny beams proudly. "I know, isn't she?"

Penny has things all planned out. She'll be going to Icana while her parents look after Olivia. It's not an ideal situation, but if anyone can handle it, I know Penny can. She has the determination to make it happen.

I haven't seen Jonah. He was arrested and charged with kidnapping and assault for what he did to me and Dayton. I heard that they also investigated him for drug offenses, but I think his father must have covered for him, because he didn't get charged for that. Instead, he served only four months in jail and was required to take anger management classes. From what I heard, he was kicked out of D-Phi, never returned to Icana, and never finished his degree. That bright future I thought he had turned out to be nothing more than an illusion. *He* was an illusion, from top to bottom, a dream I created in my head because I wanted it so badly. But I don't want it anymore. At least, not right now. I have other things I want to do first.

Still, sometimes I think I see Jonah on the street, but it's never him. I'm glad. I don't think my heart can take that.

Penny's mom picks the baby up and puts her in my arms. She weighs next to nothing, and she's just a sweet pink bundle with Penny's long eyelashes. I sigh as I look at her, thinking of Kyle. It's his loss. Judging from all the flowers and gifts that arrived for her baby shower, this baby is going to be so loved.

"Let's get a picture of you," Penny's mom says, holding up her phone, and we gather around Penny, sitting on the edge of the bed.

Penny squeezes us. "Baby Olivia and her two aunties. I couldn't have done it without you."

The mistakes we make are only the end of the story if we let them be. It's the picking up of the pieces and moving forward that makes us who we are. And right now, there is so much to celebrate.

"Say cheese!" she calls.

We all shout out, "Cheese!"

It's a great day, full of possibilities. And I can't wait for what comes next.

212

THE END

About the Author

Jessica Tondt's deep-seated passion for empowering young adults shines through her debut novel, *Meant To Be*. Drawing on her experiences as a high school and college educator, mentor, and trusted advisor, Jessica has guided countless students in discovering their passions and blossoming into their best selves.

A lifelong lover of the written word, Jessica's childhood dreams of publishing have now come to fruition. When she's not crafting stories, you can find her... well, crafting! Jessica enjoys crocheting, exploring the world through travel and hiking, experimenting in the kitchen, or enjoying walks with her dog.